Robert Wallace

Empire of Terror: Phantom Detective Saga

OK Publishing 2021

Robert Wallace
Empire of Terror: Phantom Detective Saga

Published by

MUSAICUM

Books

- Advanced Digital Solutions & High-Quality book Formatting -

musaicumbooks@okpublishing.info

2021 OK Publishing

ISBN 978-80-272-7875-6

Contents

Chapter One
Killers in Black

The bright, dazzlingly clear Arizona sky gave no hint of the ominous.

Outside the two-story frame building housing the temporary national radio network concentrated at Rock Canyon Dam, a midday sun gleamed brazenly down upon the several thousand sweltering, enthusiastic citizens and officials expectantly milling about the giant dam a half mile away.

Within the unpainted radio headquarters, on the second floor, three engineers with an assistant each, and three United States Army soldiers acting as guards under a hard-boiled infantry lieutenant, waited alertly for the hands of the electric clock on the drab wall to point to the hour of noon.

At the precise stroke of twelve the President of the United States, broadcasting in person from Rock Canyon Dam, would dedicate and formally open the greatest Federal irrigation project in the history of the country.

Lundbalm, the stocky chief radio engineer, touched a volume dial with tensed fingers and said over his hunched shoulder to Lieutenant Howard in charge of the army guards:

"Twelve minutes to go. The Marine band is hooked in now from Washington. It'll be hell if something goes wrong here."

"Nothing can go wrong," the lieutenant snapped. "This isn't the Tennessee Valley flood disaster, if that's what you're thinking of. We're prepared, this time. The entire section here is under guard. It's fool-proof!"

A frown darkened the square face of the chief engineer, and for a worried moment he stared grimly at the battery of signal lamps in a panel along one wall.

A duplicate set of signal bulbs, a brief month ago, had given him and the world the only warning of that ruthless devastation. Those lamps had flared violently a minute before the public opening of the famous Tennessee Federal power project.

Then the lights had shattered in the terrific, unexplained explosion that had blasted free the pent flood waters of the vast system and turned the valley into a torrential cataract of death.

That disaster, and others smaller but similar throughout the country, it still remained unexplained. But their origin had been traced to mysterious human hands. There, the Federal Bureau of Investigation, the G-men, had run into a blank wall. They had been stopped by a strange, impenetrable emblem —a small grey seal cut in the shape of an hour-glass, with a crimson capital "I" drawn perpendicularly through the stem.

The challenging, mystical emblem had appeared but once, pasted on the forehead of the murdered Public Works engineer in charge of the demolished Tennessee Valley Project. But the weird seal had started wild, imaginative tales of terror. And ugly, mob-inspiring rumors were persisting.

"I was out on that emergency Tennessee broadcast for two hellish weeks," Lundbalm growled dourly. "It was a ghastly experience. I'll never get over it."

"Well, it can't happen here!" Lieutenant Howard guaranteed flatly. "You tend to your gadgets. I've got us all locked in this room. Leave the protection to me."

Lundbalm reached for a phone. "I'll check again with Lewis over in the main announcer's cage at the dam." He started to plug into one of a row of connections.

His hand never finished the movement.

Behind him, from a silently opening trap in the ceiling, a yellowish egg-shaped object dropped to the floor, cracked open with a quick hissing sound. Instantly, an acrid, faintly greenish gas curled swiftly upwards, filling the long room with paralyzing, blistering fumes.

Lundbalm staggered back from the instrument table, his hands clutching his throat. He stumbled against Lieutenant Howard who was blindly trying to fire his heavy service Colt up at the hideously masked face leering down at them through the opened ceiling trap.

A black-sleeved arm laced across the opening, and a knife flashed downward through the curling, greenish vapor.

The raised Colt clattered to the floor from Lieutenant Howard's fingers as the steel blade plunged hilt deep through his neck. He fell, twisting in death, his clawing hands dragging Lundbalm's gas-strangled body down with him.

Blood spurted from his throat, spilling redly over the chief engineer's beefy back as the other radio control men and the three heavily armed soldiers collapsed and fell where they stood.

Not a strangled cry had broken the swift, silent action, so rapidly had the deadly gas choked out their lives.

A black-robed, hooded figure dropped quickly through the trap and stood reaching up, his face hidden within the startlingly weird gas mask covering his head.

"Hand it down!" he ordered in a terse, gratingly harsh voice.

The black-robed arm of a similarly hooded and masked figure reached through the hole in the ceiling, passed a round, flat leather-covered parcel into those extended hands. Then the second man swung down through the opening, dropped to the floor.

With scarcely a glance at the ten dead engineers and soldiers sprawled in grotesquely pitiful huddles about the room, the two robed figures crossed wordlessly to the control switchboard. Working with expert speed, one of them disconnected several wires while the other opened the flat leather case, removed from it a black wax radio recording disc.

The first man turned abruptly, strode directly to a far corner of the long room, and came back carrying a standard studio electric portable phonograph. He hooked it up to the broadcast wires he had unfastened, glanced briefly at the wall clock, and put the black wax record on the machine.

"Good timing," his rasping voice commented. "One minute to twelve!"

His fingers flicked beneath his robe, came out holding a single small grey seal. Its design was an hour-glass, and a blood-red capital "I" was drawn upright through the stem.

He stepped quickly over to the body of Lieutenant Howard, moistened the back of the strange emblem with the army officer's blood, stuck the mysterious seal on the dead man's forehead.

His movements were swift, nerveless, as devoid of emotion as though he'd merely hurriedly pasted a stamp on a letter. He stepped back to the instrument desk, started the phonograph disc revolving, and poised the sensitive reproducing needle above the fine outer lines at the edge of the record.

"The President's uninvited ghost goes on the air in exactly thirty-five seconds," he said with low-voiced, exultant grimness.

The second robed figure, standing ready with one hand on a master-control switch, asked in a flat, dried voice:

"You sure we can get out of here all right?"

"Yellow?" Sneering contempt grated in the first man's quick, snarling retort. "The Imperator's experts never miss! We'll walk out, you fool, like ministering monks in the confusion when the dam blows!"

Slowly, nervelessly, the needle lowered toward the ominously whirling black record —A half mile away, at Rock Canyon Dam, the sweltering crowds shuffled restlessly in the hot noonday sun that beat down upon the colorful pageantry.

Enormous American flags draped the sheer walls of the gigantic dam, ready to be raised majestically on gaily bannered wires when the sluices opened at the President's pressure on an electric control key. The President himself, with his chosen administration officials and vigilant Secret-Service guards occupied a temporary, flag-draped stand in a niche cut into the rock wall above the dam.

From the horns of the public address system the National Anthem, played by the Marine Band in the nation's capital, swayed the eager watchers crowding the canyon's rugged, railed rim, and poured inspiringly from the radios of millions of listeners.

The Arlington-timed clock in the main announcer's cage at the near end of the dam showed ten seconds to noon. Mort Lewis, the veteran radio announcer, nodded to Toby, his assistant, and leaned tensely close to his microphone.

As the final rousing strains of the Marine Band faded, Lewis' clear baritone voice came over the air and through the canyon speakers along the rocky walls:

> "And now, ladies and gentlemen of America, the nation's Chief Executive is about to speak from Rock Canyon Dam-the President of the United States!"

A pause. Then the President's kindly, sincerely convincing voice: "My friends —"

Without warning, the President's voice was cut off by a sharp, amplified click.

For a bare fraction of a second there was a scratching sound, followed instantly by a swift, brassy, metallic flow of startling words:

> "This is the Imperator of the Two Americas speaking for the citizens of the rising Invisible Empire! Rock Canyon Dam, a futile project of a weak, incipient government, will be destroyed by explosives in exactly one hundred seconds. Future public disasters will follow until the purpose of constructive anarchy has been attained. Sixty seconds now remain before the explosion. I, the Imperator, have spoken!"

The chilling, metallic voice stopped with a clipped snap that was like a hammer blow on glass.

For a terrifying, suspended moment dead silence fell upon the air and gripped the assembled officials and spectators at Rock Canyon in a paralysis of helpless dread. Then pandemonium broke loose.

The crowds surged back away from the canyon's railed rim-fighting, shouting, cursing. Army officers, soldiers and state police rallied vainly to direct a swift, safe escape for the hysteria-crazed mauling mob.

Women and children were trampled underfoot. Strong men were knocked down by the wild, blundering rush. Screams drowned out the frantically shouted commands of the officers.

Three Secret Service guards grabbed the President bodily, rushed him back off the platform, hurried him out into a cleared roadway where they, with the willing help of his official party, made a white-faced, desperately protecting ring with their bodies.

Down on the rim of the dam, Mort Lewis shouted futilely into his dead mike in a frantic, heroic attempt to direct the crowd caught and jammed in the lower approaches. He waved Toby, his assistant, toward the exit bored into the canyon wall, rushed after him at the last second.

The veteran announcer was three yards from the narrow exit when the first terrific detonation rocked the canyon from deep in the bowels of the mighty dam. The rock walls trembled.

He stared down, hypnotized into rigidity by the enormous snake-like cracks appearing in a patternless maze across the solid face of the man-made water barrier. The greenish expanse of imprisoned flood, extending for miles back of the dam, rippled and shuddered.

And suddenly, as a second shock reverberated, Lewis' widened eyes narrowed on the black-hooded, cloaked figures emerging from a leaking sluice slot at the dam's base, running for shelter. A moment later, with three more thunderous explosions shattering the masonry, the center of the dam split open into an enormous, writhing V.

A harsh, angry roar arose drowning out the rumble of the rocking blasts, and the strangled water poured through the split, tearing away huge pieces of the dam, widening the vital opening.

The two fleeing black-robed figures disappeared, whirled away in the first rush of the flood that blotted out the power houses and buildings at the foot of the dam as though by, magic in a hellish cataract of thundering destruction.

The churning water rushed on, sweeping everything in its path. The helpless spectators, workmen and soldiers caught beneath the rising tide of the whirling, serpentine monster of death, were gone like straws, their despairing cries lost utterly in the horrifying roar of the plunging flood.

Mort Lewis swayed dizzily, leaped for the dangerous safety of the narrow exit at the end of the completely crumpling dam. He lunged halfway through the tunnel opening, was knocked down as part of the wall gave way.

Rocks and shale pounded down on his twisted legs, pinioned him helplessly to the stone floor. He lay there writhing, sweating in agony, while behind him the snarling torrent drowned out his shouting, fading voice.

Chapter Two
Red Warning

Lowering purplish storm clouds had hovered menacingly over New York City all day, seemingly caught and held stationary by the sharp spires and pinnacles of the towering skyscrapers. At three o'clock in the afternoon the storm hadn't broken yet, and the spasmodic rumble of thunder was just beginning to become annoying over radios in crackling static.

But it wasn't storm interference that broke in upon the swing music floating from the hidden radio in the large Moorish reception room of the stately Fifth Avenue residence of Mr. Frank Havens, the nationally known publisher. It was the announcer's smooth voice cutting in from Radio City:

> "Ladies and gentlemen, through the facilities of the National Broadcasting Company, you are about to hear the President of the United States speak from Rock Canyon Dam, Arizona, where he will formally open the largest irrigation system in the world. One moment, please —"

As the fading strains of the National Anthem, played by the U. S. Marine Band, swelled into the big, gaily crowded reception room, Muriel Havens stopped dancing and smiled whimsically up into the lean, tanned face of Richard Curtis Van Loan.

"Something official like that would have to break into my afternoon tea-dance," she protested with a little laugh, and started to signal a butler to dial in another program.

Dick Van Loan stopped her with a quick shake of his head and moved with her nearer the wide window where the radio was camouflaged in a flower-covered wall table.

"Mind if I listen to him?" he asked politely, and added, "The daughter of Frank Havens should be able to inflict the President's voice on her guests for a few min —"

His bantering words broke off abruptly as his sharp eyes flicked to the window.

Out across Central Park, rising high above the skyscrapers of the Roaring Forties to the south, blinking red lights on Frank Havens' towering Clarion Press Building gleamed now, flashing warningly, vividly against the purplish background of foreboding storm clouds.

The Phantom's signal! Neither exclamation nor tremor betrayed the vitalizing shock that whipped Dick Van Loan's nerves into tensed alertness. His signal-from Frank Havens-Around him the gay party went on, heedless and merrily ignorant of the dire call. Even Muriel Havens, the nationally powerful publisher's beautiful daughter, had no inkling of the grim Phantom drama being signaled in by those rapidly winking lights atop her father's Clarion tower.

Dick Van Loan's cryptic smile gave no hint of the driving turmoil seething within him as he deciphered that flashing code message:

> Calling the Phantom-Come to my office —
> Hurry-This is a murder call-Havens —
> Calling the Phantom —

The dots and dashes kept on winking ominously, would continue to blink that secret message until the Phantom himself contacted Frank Havens. Van Loan damned himself mentally. He'd been idling here, dancing, unalert to that urgent message.

But before his brain could hit upon an acceptably logical excuse to offer Muriel Havens for an abrupt departure, the familiar voice of the veteran radio announcer, Mort Lewis, broke in upon his consciousness:

> "—From Rock Canyon Dam-The President of the United States!"

Then the President's warm voice: "My friends —"

Dick Van Loan's eyes narrowed at the sharp click that interrupted the President's kindly greeting.

The next instant, as the first chilling words of that strange unannounced metallic voice came brassily over the air, Van stooped low over the radio table, his tensed fingers twisting off the volume. He motioned Muriel Havens away, dialed the icy flow of words until he alone in the room could hear:

" —the Imperator of the Two Americas speaking for the Invisible Empire. Rock Canyon Dam will be destroyed in-one hundred seconds. Future public disasters will follow-Sixty seconds —I, the Imperator, have spoken!"

Grimly, his knuckles white against the dial, Dick Van Loan spun the volume on full as the icy metallic voice stopped with a brittle snap that was like glass broken by a hammer blow. But now only a vague rumbling sound and the crackle of distant static came from the suddenly stilled station.

Tight-lipped, Van turned down the power to normal volume, dialed in a dance orchestra on a minor local station, and rose to face Muriel. No use disrupting her afternoon party with this new, grimly spectacular radio mystery. Damage enough, that millions of listeners had heard that dire, threatening voice.

"Something went wrong with the President's address," he said to her with a convincing smile of apology.

"I'm a very hard-boiled stockholder in that broadcasting company, so you won't mind. Muriel, if I run off from your very pleasant soiree to see what's happened?"

How much she minded was evident in her gently veiled, disappointed gaze as she let him go. But it was not a polite lie that Dick Van Loan used to excuse himself from the Havens home.

He did own stock in the National Broadcasting Company. In a number of other industrial corporations, too. And in Frank Havens' coast-to-coast chain of newspapers, including the New York Clarion. Richard Curtis Van Loan was wealthy, but not cumbersomely so.

But the tall, athletic Park Avenue clubman and man-about-town had cleared his mind of Muriel's tea-dance before he reached the curb. And he had no intention of driving first to Radio City, as he jumped into his fast, powerful coupe. South of Central Park, the Clarion tower lights were still flashing their urgent secret code for the Phantom.

And the Phantom was answering that call! Answering it now in the fast run of Dick Van Loan's dark blue coupe down Fifth Avenue and across town to Eighth.

He parked a block from the towering Clarion Press building, but did not immediately get out of the car. Instead, bending low in the coupe's seat, he produced from a panel beneath him a small, compactly equipped make-up kit.

Working rapidly, with swift glances of caution at the hurrying pedestrians passing a few feet from the car windows, he began the familiar task of disguising his features. It was an old story with him, this quick change of character.

Always, when the inevitable Clarion call came to war on crime, it was Van's deft, experienced fingers that brought the Phantom into being again-as those sure, artistic fingers had done in the beginning. For the Phantom was Dick Van Loan's own creation, a product of his restless energy, his fearless demand for action, and his determination to put his wealth and talents to the best use.

Van hated crime and criminals instinctively. But it was Frank Havens, a far older man, who had shown him that always, behind the scenes of every series of modern crimes, some one brain, some one man, was the ruthless guiding genius, untouchable by the usual forces of law or the police.

The Phantom was Richard Curtis Van Loan's answer to the death challenge of lawlessness. The Phantom, a sinister figure without name, without identity-more untouchable and grimly mysterious than the slipperiest of those crooks and killer geniuses of crime whose ravages he was fighting.

It was the Phantom's real identity, the identity of Richard Curtis Van Loan behind the varied character disguises of the Phantom, that had to be ultimately and desperately protected.

16

Without that complete anonymity, all the aids he used-the different character roles, the three hideouts, his gift of ventriloquism, even the red code lights still signalling him from the pinnacle of the Clarion Building-went for naught.

Dick Van Loan slid the make-up case under the seat into its trick compartment. But it wasn't the Park Avenue clubman who sat upright in the coupe now.

The lean, tanned face had disappeared, replaced by a square featured, sallow-skinned man twenty years older than Van Loan. The hair was combed unbecomingly on the opposite side of the greying head, and the eyebrows curled upward belligerently.

A twist of the necktie, a slip of two notches in the soft leather belt, and an awkward, ill-fitting hitch of the grey suit coat, rounded out the convincing picture of a rugged, aggressive but personally sloppy and rather shopworn character of no particular qualifications.

What unknown talents the character possessed, were added to by a shoulder-holstered Colt .38 automatic, a carefully pocketed black silk mask, a pencil flashlight, and a peculiarly designed platinum and diamond badge.

It was seventeen minutes after three o'clock in the afternoon, and the delayed storm was just beginning to spatter the pavement with the first big drops of a heavy rain, when the Phantom, alias Jim Doran, jammed a crumpled panama low over his eyes and faded down the street away from the locked coupe.

He paused abruptly at the corner of Eighth Avenue, lighted a cigarette as he listened to an announcer's tense voice cracking from a loudspeaker in a radio shop doorway:

> "Flash! The giant government irrigation project at Rock Canyon Dam, Arizona, has just been destroyed by a series of devastating explosions. The entire dam has been demolished and the canyon itself is a raging torrent. Loss of life is estimated at well over a thousand, with the toll mounting.

> "Property damage will be incalculable until the water now sweeping the whole Arizona valley spends itself. The President of the United States was saved by quick action on the part of his Secret Service guards and members of his staff. This report comes by telephone from Phoenix, all radio facilities at Rock Canyon having been destroyed by the disastrous explosions.

> "A mysterious voice, cutting in upon the President's dedicatory address at the dam a few seconds before the series of blasts, threatened this fatal national disaster and others to follow.

> "Federal investigators are flying to the scene. This is the first report that has been received. More details will be broadcast as they are relayed to us."

The voice stopped, and people on the street stared blankly at one another, stunned, heedless of the increasing rain.

Jim Doran's squarish face became rocky, his keen grey eyes smoldering as he strode grimly a half block north. He ducked into a subway kiosk, came up into the Clarion Building on the other side of the wet street.

The Phantom was reborn.

Chapter Three
Special Corpse

The editorial offices of the Clarion were on the eleventh floor and Frank Havens had a bullet-proof glass cubicle there, raised above the floor level in a far corner.

But the publisher's real office was a triplex suite on the eighty-fifth and top floors of the towering press building, reached only by a private express elevator entered through a sliding panel in that non-shatterable glass cubicle overlooking the editorial rooms.

Turmoil and cyclonic confusion seemed to have hit the enormous editorial office when Jim Doran stepped off the public elevator and was stopped by the wise-eyed blond receptionist at the railing gate. Telephones jangled, typewriters and teletypes clattered, adding to the bedlam of excitedly shouted orders and rushing copy boys.

But the suspense-ridden, grinding overtones of the Clarion's frenzied editorial department, the Phantom realized grimly, was only a larger duplicate, of the frantic commotion occurring in every metropolitan press editorial room in the country at this moment. The universal, terse newspaper cry was:

Hold that Rock Canyon wire open!

"Jim Doran, to see Mr. Frank Havens," Van told the girl curtly. Jim Doran was one of the score of names that Dick Van Loan and the publisher had agreed upon as Phantom aliases. "Mr. Havens is expecting me," he added as the girl at the desk hesitated.

She gave him a sharp, respectfully curious glance as she finished putting through the call to Havens' quarters, and a moment later Jim Doran was slouching through the familiar maze of editorial desks, guided by an alert copy boy.

Toby, the publisher's trusted elevator guard, rode him up in the private express car from the glass cubicle, watching him warily but without recognition. Toby had known Richard Curtis Van Loan for some years.

Van's veiled grey eyes hid his satisfaction, as the keen scrutiny of the operator failed to catch the slightest flaw in the quick character make-up of nondescript Jimmy Doran. Toby's shrewd, bold eyes were always an infallible first test.

At the eighty-fifth floor, the swarthy operator slid back the elevator door. Jim Doran stepped out of the car, stood a moment in the ornately furnished reception foyer staring belligerently at the uniformed policeman eyeing him suspiciously. Behind him, the car door slid shut silently as Toby took the elevator down again.

"I'm here to see Mr. Havens," Van announced in a deep, gruff voice that was not at all the smooth baritone of Richard Curtis Van Loan. "Didn't expect to find you cops up here."

Before the policeman could question him, Judkins' tall, bald-headed figure appeared on a balcony at one end of the room. The publisher's confidential secretary called down to the cop:

"If that's Mr. Doran, send him right up, officer."

Van nodded to the cop, brushed past him and mounted the staircase to the balcony.

Judkins' sallow glance was nervous but his worried brown eyes were without recognition as he led Jim Doran through a doorway into a large room that was more lounge than office.

"Mr. James Doran," he announced, and withdrew, closing the door.

Frank Havens' penetrating gaze darted up sharply as Dick Van Loan crossed to the wide, polished walnut desk behind which the publisher sat drumming his fingers anxiously. Six other men, one in the uniform of a police captain, looked up quickly from the armchair about which they were grouped.

But the figure slumped in that chair did not move.

As Van's swift glance took in the unusual tableau, his right hand swung across the desk toward Havens in a hearty handshake that hid the small platinum-and-diamond badge palmed in his long fingers. The significant emblem of a mask outlined by the brilliant gems was the only design on the smooth platinum surface of that cryptic shield. But it was enough.

Frank Havens' worried eyes glinted with recognition as Van's swift fingers gave him, but not the others, a flashing look at that Phantom badge. The emblem disappeared again in Jim Doran's hand.

"Gentlemen, Mr. James Doran!" Havens said and stood up from behind his desk. The name had weight now as he spoke it. Jim Doran was no longer a password name, but had become a reality. "Mr. Doran will represent me in this investigation." He nodded his grey head toward the silent figure in the armchair.

Van stepped over to the armchair, his eyes on the domelike head of the middle-aged man slumped there. A small fleck of blood stained the fellow's white lips as the Phantom raised the lolling head and studied the fixed expression of sheer surprise stamped on the dead man's face.

Rigor mortis had not yet set in, and there were no visible marks of violence on the neatly dressed body.

"This wants some preliminary explaining," Jim Doran grumbled. "I didn't think anybody'd be interested in just one corpse, after what happened at Rock Creek Canyon."

"We know about that," the officer in the captain's uniform said. "This happens to be New York City, not Arizona."

Van glanced up, curiously aware that Havens, in his repressed excitement, had not named him as the Phantom, although two of the men in street clothes were obviously homicide detectives.

The other three men in the room were big, well dressed fellows. Frank Havens made the brief introductions.

One of the strangers was Warden Jack Bluebold of Alleghany Penitentiary at Mountainview, Pennsylvania. The next man was Dr. Maurice Jessup, resident surgeon at the Alleghany prison. The third was ex-Congressman Harry Arnold, a Pennsylvania politician. The three of them stayed close together in a compact, capable group.

Havens eyed the lifeless figure in the armchair, frowned and said:

> "Lester Gimble is-was-one of the leading metallurgists in this country. Because I wanted an article on the subject, I induced him to interview Dr. Waldo Junes, the famous scientist who is conducting some unusual experiments in metals at the General Electric laboratory at Niagara Falls. Gimble was on his way back here —"

Havens broke off, nodded to the plainclothes men.

"Simmons and me," the taller of the two dicks said, jerking his head at his partner, "were standing in Grand Central Station near the taxicab entrance about two-thirty this afternoon, when this fellow Gimble shows with a suitcase and a briefcase, coming from the lower level train platforms.

"He starts to get into a cab, when two guys take a shot at him from behind. He dropped his bags and swung round. One of the gunmen grabs up his suitcase and the other one got the briefcase. Simmons and me opened up on 'em then and there was a hell of a lot of racket and commotion.

"I killed the bird with the suitcase before he got ten steps, but the one with the briefcase got into the crowd where Simmons didn't dare shoot. So far as we heard yet, the second guy got away. A lot of cops were after him by that time, so Simmons and me took care of this Gimble who'd been shot at.

"He claimed he wasn't either hit or hurt, and had to get over here to see Mr. Havens in a hurry —" The tall detective shrugged and glanced deprecatingly at Captain Walters.

"Well, we knew who Mr. Havens was, so we took Gimble and his suitcase and brought him over here."

Frank Havens nodded. "The right thing to do, under the circumstances." His blue, penetrating eyes swung to the Phantom. "Mr. Gimble came in here with these two officers and sat down in the chair he's in now, he hadn't said anything on the short ride over, and he was looking rather white. Before he had a chance to talk, he slumped over and died.

"I had the Clarion's staff physician rush right up here from downstairs, but nothing could be done. We found that Gimble had been shot in the spine."

"That's why we didn't see any blood," Detective Simmons stated. "Them kind of wounds don't hardly bleed at all, and the victim don't feel he's been shot because he's numbed. He don't die until the fluid in the spine drains out like an internal hemorrhage. But how was we to know —"

"The Clarion physician exonerated both of you," Havens declared. "I've heard of similar cases, particularly during the war. Gimble would have died anyway. But what are we going to do now?"

He turned to Van. "I phoned for Captain Walters and asked him to keep this free of the regular police routine for one hour. I'm glad you got here so quickly, Mr. Doran."

"If you haven't found anything of importance in Gimble's suitcase, or on his person, and if that scientist, Dr. Junes up in Niagara Falls, can't give you a lead of some sort," Van growled, "you don't need any help until the police catch the gunman who got away with Gimble's brief-case." He shot a look at Captain Walters. "That is, unless the man this detective killed can be identified."

"We're working on that angle," Walters snapped, and said pointedly to Havens, "If it's okay now, let's have the Homicide Squad and the Medical Examiner in on this."

Havens eyed Van questioningly, and when Jim Doran nodded, the precinct captain picked up the phone, asked for Headquarters.

"There was absolutely nothing in Gimble's pockets, nor in his suitcase, that points to a clue," Havens said emphatically. "We went through everything while we were waiting for you. And I've put a call through to the General Electric Experimental Laboratory, but Dr. Junes refuses to be disturbed and won't answer the phone."

He motioned Van to follow him across the large room to a teletype machine in the corner. The tape, twisting snakelike over the rim of the overflowing receptacle, was still uncoiling the grim account of the life and property toll at Rock Canyon Dam.

Havens fingered the ticker-tape with a trembling hand, looked searchingly at the Phantom. "I didn't tell them" —he nodded toward the three police officers, and lowered his voice —"who you were, because I thought you'd want to work on that Arizona disaster, Van."

Jim Doran's slatey eyes were inscrutable. "I saw the Clarion tower lights signaling just before the N.B.C. network started to put the President on the air. Yes, Frank," he agreed in a grave, low-pitched tone, "I'd like to go after the brain that is directing these catastrophes. I heard his voice-if that was his voice, making that threat over the radio. Somebody will have to stop him!"

The Phantom looked keenly at the famous publisher. Havens was staring out through the wide windows overlooking Manhattan and the New Jersey hills green against the background of dark, scudding rain clouds. The older man's blue, moody eyes seemed to be envisaging the calamity that threatened those peaceful, rolling lands and the vast country beyond, presaged in the thin, endless record of the tape sliding implacably through his fingers.

"Somebody must stop him!" Havens repeated with a note of despair in the almost-whispered words.

Van asked shrewdly, "What did you send Gimble to Niagara for, Frank? It wasn't just a news article you wanted!"

"You're right," Havens confessed. "Dr. Junes is trying to unite two metals, aluminum and calbite, heretofore impossible of fusion because high enough temperatures couldn't be reached. It's an experiment a lot of steel and munitions manufacturers would like to know about.

"If those two metals can be fused, the result will be the most impenetrable armorplate in the world, a new metal ten thousand times harder and stronger than the toughest of modern steels!"

"At least tough enough to get Lester Gimble murdered," Van commented, and glanced at the three big men from Pennsylvania. "What are those fellows here for?"

"Ex-Congressman Arnold came here with the other two prison officials to ask me to stop giving publicity in my newspapers to the graft and corruption that's been reported at Alleghany

Penitentiary. They were here when Gimble came in. Harry Arnold is chairman of the Pennsylvania Board of Parole and Pardons. He and Bluebold and Jessup claim the publicity I've been giving their prison has interfered with their attempts to ferret out and clean up the prison rottenness. I'm convinced they're right, too."

Van nodded, and said to Havens as the police captain called to them, "Keep the Phantom out of this, Frank, until I tell you otherwise."

Captain Walters had finished phoning, with flustering results.

"A sour mess this is turning out to be!" he exclaimed. "Doran, you wanted to get a line on that bird Jackson, the detective, killed."

Van's voice slipped into character again, became a harsh, demanding growl.

"If it's a lead, hand it out," he grumbled.

"It's a lead that's going to raise hell over in Pennsylvania," Walters declared. "That gunman Jackson shot is Snakey Willow, a lifer at Alleghany Penitentiary!"

The three brawny prison officials eyeing Captain Walters glanced sharply over to Frank Havens and Jim Doran.

"Snakey Willow —" Warden Bluebold's voice was a dry rasp. "He was in the prison three days ago, when we left. By —"

"Yeah," Walters said caustically. "He ain't there now! And I didn't see any police teleflash about his escape yet, neither. But that's not all. The rogues gallery picture of him we had at Headquarters don't fit his face. He had a fresh operation on his mug! If he'd been able to erase his fingerprints, we'd never have found out who he was!"

Dr. Maurice Jessup, the prison's resident surgeon, frowned, and glanced sharply at Bluebold. "I don't think the report you received is correct. Not in intent, anyway, sir. I remember Willow —I should, because he had an accident in the prison foundry and I operated to save his life. His face was very badly burned, so I did my best to patch it up. If that's what you refer to, Captain."

"Well," Walters said grudgingly, "that's different!"

Harry Arnold, the ex-congressman from Pennsylvania, broke in with, "It's a mistake that Willow was able to escape at all! Mr. Havens, you can see the state things are in at Alleghany Prison. If there's any more adverse publicity, we're apt to have a prison riot or an organized jailbreak. If you'll give us some help, by stopping advertising the conditions, I'll guarantee the prison is cleaned up!"

"You're right, Mr. Arnold," Havens said determinedly. "I'll do my best to keep this escape quiet. But see that the prison is reorganized at once, or I'll have to expose the whole situation, and you're apt to have the Federal Prison authorities step in!"

Jim Doran's slatey eyes had become the color of muddy marble. He nodded abruptly to the men in the office. "The police can handle this. I'll get the details later from them," he announced curtly, and strode out of the room.

But only Frank Havens caught and appreciated the determined, eager gleam that had crept into Jim Doran's sardonic gaze.

Several police officials, two internes and a man from the medical examiner's office were waiting in the bulletproof glass cubicle down on the eleventh floor when Van got out of the elevator. The editorial room was still a bedlam of cyclonic confusion.

Out on Eighth Avenue a persistent rain was wetting the shouted Clarion extras:

TITANIC EXPLOSIONS WRECK
HUGE FEDERAL PROJECT

Weird Radio Voice Threatens Further Disasters

Chapter Four
Dread Snatch

Snakey Willow's body lay flat and deflated on the cold morgue slab when Van pulled back the disinfected white sheet and bent close over the dead killer's wax-like face. Even in death, the escaped murderer's features were menacing and evil.

Special attention had evidently been given Snakey Willow's face-lifting operation by the Bellevue Hospital medicos, for the recently healed incisions under the tight-skinned jowls and along the high cheekbones had been slit open again by the autopsy scalpels.

Studying those freshly reopened incisions keenly the Phantom smiled thinly to himself.

He was no M.D., but mechanized crime hunts had led him deeply into the study of modern drugs, hypnosis and medicine. He recognized here, in Snakey Willow's now mutilated features, the sensitive hand of an exceptionally fine surgeon.

The criminal's nose had been remoulded, shortened and widened in a manner that tended to broaden the appearance of the unchangeable bone structure of the narrow head. No wonder the sharp eyes of the New York City police had failed to recognize that revamped face.

But it was the deft, startlingly liberal application of skin grafting that held the Phantom's concentrated attention. He fingered a small, powerful magnifying glass from his vest pocket, focused it upon those hundreds of individual skin grafts that had covered the incisions of the original plastic surgery operation.

Each graft, he knew, had been a separate detail taking time and infinite patience-and taking, also, a dangerously large amount of live skin.

Van pulled the white sheet all the way off the nude figure, examined the body carefully from shoulders to feet for scars of skin removal. He found none, and slid the sheet back up over the corpse slowly, his grey eyes moody and thoughtful.

Some other person had provided the live skin for this facial operation. And from the amount of skin grafted, it had been a dangerous venture for the donor.

Snakey Willow was not a type to have sacrificing friends. And prison hospitals didn't provide such donations for convicts. Somebody had been paid a big sum for the skin used. Or else force had been used to take it.

Before Jim Doran replaced the magnifying glass in his pocket, he examined the dead man's fingertips. They had been tampered with, showed the marks of acid burns, but the tell-tale whorls had not been eradicated.

Even skin grafting could not stop those true fingerprints from growing back again to identify their owner. Snakey Willow had, it seemed, tried to polish off for criminally practical purposes a job the prison surgeon had done to save his life.

Van Loan left the Bellevue morgue with three convictions:

The prison surgeon who had repaired Snakey Willow's face had performed one of the finest technical and artistic operations the Phantom had ever seen. The skin grafting job had taken more live epidermis than any one donor could safely give. And the entire operation had cost far more money than Snakey Willow could ever have paid.

Beyond those three conclusions the Phantom refused to confuse his mind with speculation. He made a phone call from a drug store booth to his garage, asking that his coupe be picked up near the Clarion Building.

A second telephone message got Wild Jerry Lannigan at the mid-town apartment where the Phantom kept sanctuary quarters under Lannigan's name.

"Holmes Airport at eight this evening, Champ," he said curtly when the big red-headed man's voice boomed over the wire. "We're flying the Beechcraft to Buffalo."

At the other end of the line he could hear Jerry Lannigan's explosive exclamation of enthusiasm. "Champ" was the familiar name that only the Phantom used for the beefy, reckless ex-army mechanic and pilot. It served as a confidential and friendly identification, for not even Lannigan knew the Phantom was Richard Van Loan.

"Okay, Skipper!" Lannigan was too close to Van personally to use The Phantom appellation, and too smart to bandy it over a public phone. "The ship'll be gassed and oiled. It's about time something happened. I heard that guy with the screwy voice break in on the President's radio broadcast —"

Van cut him off with a cryptic, "So did too many other people, Champ. The man at the airport will be Professor Bendix," and hung up.

The Jim Doran disguise had sufficed for the hurried Phantom appearance at the Clarion, but a character of far more ponderance would be needed for the difficult interview Van planned. And there was some special technical information he wanted before he visited Dr. Waldo Junes at the General Electric Experimental Laboratory at Niagara Falls.

The place to effect both of these needs was in the seclusion of that sound- and explosion-proof lab in the old abandoned river-front building up on the East Side.

There was nothing of the scientist in the appearance of the slouching figure of Jim Doran as he swung off a First Avenue bus at Ninetieth Street and ambled with wary carelessness toward the East River.

At the dock end of the street a deserted red brick warehouse loomed on the left, its dirty windows staring vacuously through the still drizzling rain of the late summer afternoon. Jim Doran paused as he reached the corner of the decrepit building, glanced furtively about him.

The next instant he had faded into the darker shadows beneath the dilapidated loading platform.

A gaping, broken coal-chute window let him drop through into the darkness of the warehouse basement. He crossed the musty concrete floor with quick, familiar steps, produced a small brass key from a hidden crevice in the masonry at the opposite end of the silent cellar.

A moment later and he'd unlocked and pulled open a heavy counter-balanced steel and concrete trap door in the floor.

The Phantom lowered himself down a metal ladder, closed the trap above him, locked it and snapped on a light switch. He stood in the large steel-walled sub-cellar laboratory of Professor Paul Bendix.

Three-quarters of the long, low-ceilinged chamber was equipped with indestructible work tables upon which were an array of glass jars, racks of test tubes, Bunsen burners, heat-resisting crocks. A large electric arc furnace filled one corner of the modern lab. And along two walls were rows of compactly stacked shelves of chemical supplies.

The remaining quarter of the long room was a well stocked scientific library of modern chemistry, physics and crime literature in bound volumes, in professional technical magazines, and in those privately printed abstruse brochures published by the more learned scientific societies for purposes of research. The library represented seven languages.

There were no windows in the room, but a hidden ventilation system operating through a disused chimney in the warehouse tended to the air and chemical fumes when Professor Bendix used the laboratory. Behind a screen in a corner of the library was a couch, a dressing table, a shower and a large steel wardrobe case with a combination lock.

Jim Doran stepped over to that wardrobe, unlocked and opened it with four deft turns of the dial.

Inside hung an array of clothes-the rough garments of Gunner McGlone, a Chinatown character as mysterious as he was tough; the loud-checked suit of Lucky Luke Lamar, the swaggering gambler; the tuxedo and dinner clothes of Maxie Herman the Hermit, a unique Broadway figure who emerged bat-like from some undiscovered seclusion to frequent the night clubs, cabarets and expensive gambling and vice dens of Manhattan after dark.

There, too, hung the greenish, antique frock coat, the wing-collared shirt and the baggy striped trousers of that strange, erratically brilliant scientist, Professor Paul Bendix, the owner of this underground laboratory.

A brief smile of appreciation curved Dick Van Loan's lips as his grey eyes slid over that array of garments.

He touched the sleeve of Maxie the Hermit's tuxedo reminiscently.

The last time he'd worn that disguise, the Hermit had exchanged hot lead with Trigger Dwyer, now dead, across the crooked roulette table of the extinct Gold Casino Club.

The Phantom's smile faded, shutting out the past. This was a grimmer case he was facing. The tough disguise of Gunner McGlone might prove more appropriate in combating the murderer of Lester Gimble. But right now Professor Paul Bendix was needed.

He took down the faded, greenish frock coat and the rest of the professor's eccentric, old-fashioned clothes. From the bottom of the steel wardrobe cabinet he lifted a metal make-up box, opened it on the mirror-backed dressing table.

Sitting before the triple mirror, with a strong electric light focusing his reflection, the Phantom's trained fingers went to work. Jim Doran disappeared, became Richard Curtis Van Loan again.

Then the lean, tanned face of the Park Avenue clubman faded rapidly beneath the squarish, bearded features of Professor Bendix.

Fifteen minutes later the Phantom closed and locked the steel cabinet and adjusted the worn frock coat on his padded shoulders.

Professor Bendix was a big man physically as well as scientifically, and spoke with a slightly guttural accent. Van made a few practise gestures before the mirrors, then turned to the shelves of specialized technical books and magazines.

For a solid hour he pored over involved treatises dealing with metallurgy and explosives. Rock Canyon Dam was supposed to have been engineered to withstand even T.N.T. and the newer picric acid explosive compounds.

And for another hour he studied various medical journals, confining his research to articles on plastic surgery and skin grafting. Dr. Jessup's operation on Willow might not have been a matter of sheer coincidence.

By seven o'clock he was finished, his mind a bit fagged from the strain of such continuous concentration. But his confidence was backed now by definite knowledge of the specialized and seemingly unrelated subjects he appeared to be up against.

He let himself out of the laboratory through the heavy steel door that opened directly onto the stubby concrete dock jutting out into the East River. Van had bought and equipped this abandoned warehouse under the name of Paul Bendix, so in character he was free to come and go as he chose, without the handicap of secrecy —a stooped, hulking and harmless old gentleman steeped in abstract problems of pure science.

He phoned Frank Havens from a booth, caught him still in the Clarion office, and identified himself with a clipped: "Jim Doran."

"I'm going to Niagara, flying with the Champ," he said cryptically. "Dr. Bendix. But unannounced, Frank. Anything new come up?"

Haven's voice was irritable with worry. "Yes. Mort Lewis, the radio announcer at Rock Canyon, was the last man alive off the dam. He was found partially buried in a tunnel exit, but was revived. He reports that two men wearing black robes and black hoods ran out of the bottom of the dam after the first two explosions, and were drowned in the flood. Several soldiers claim they saw two similarly robed figures walking away from the building there that was used for the radio control station. Every man in that radio station was murdered, including the guards!"

The Phantom whistled tunelessly through clamped teeth. Havens' voice went on:

"Somebody tried unsuccessfully to break into the ore exhibit of the Smithsonian Institute at Washington, D. C., last night. An F.B.I. man has been added to the building's regular watchmen.

"How do you figure a connection?" Van asked. "The Smithsonian is a long jump from a revival of the Ku Klux idea in Arizona."

"I'm not figuring," Havens' voice snapped, and the publisher added apologetically a moment later, "It's only that I know Dr. Junes visited the Smithsonian a month ago and was given a chip off a meteoric fragment on display there. He was using it, how I don't know, in his Niagara experiments with aluminum and calbite. I rather expected you'd go out to that Alleghany Penitentiary, after finding Willow had escaped."

"There's the two choices," the Phantom explained. "Remember, Gimble was murdered evidently for information he'd got from Dr. Junes. If I can see Junes first, I might have something positive to work on from the prison angle, afterward. You'll hear from me."

He hung up. Out on the street, he bought a late Clarion extra. The dam disaster in Arizona, the headlines screamed, was still spreading destruction through the lower valley of the enormous Federal project.

Arizona state militia had taken charge of the paralyzed flood district, and the Federal Bureau of Investigation had a number of men on the job. But as yet nothing definite had been unearthed regarding either the mechanics of the terrific explosion, or the fiendish operators who had set off those devastating blasts.

On a back page, crowded in with the comparatively inconsequential local news, was a short item about the shooting that afternoon in Grand Central Station. It was given out that Lester Gimble had died suddenly on his way home from the attack, with a bullet lodged in his spine, But the fact that he had actually died in the Clarion Press Building was omitted.

The motive was given as probably robbery.

Professor Paul Bendix left the newspaper on the counter of a diner where he ate a hurried meal, and climbed into a taxi. As the cab rolled over Queensboro Bridge toward Holmes Airport, the nearest aviation field on Long Island, the cab radio began announcing late news.

The Phantom listened moodily to more flood reports from the Arizona area. But suddenly his eyes narrowed as a flash announcement came over the air:

> Niagara Falls, New York. Dr. Waldo Junes, noted chemical scientist conducting secret metallurgical experiments in the General Electric Research Laboratories in that city, was driven from his underground workshop late this afternoon by an explosion that demolished a portion of the laboratory and wrecked his experiment. The Doctor is at home, recovering from shock, and claims he cannot explain the cause of the blast, but will never attempt the experiment again that he was conducting, because of the danger to humanity —a danger which he also refuses to explain.

Professor Paul Bendix leaned forward in the cab seat, his grey eyes sharp and penetrating beneath their shaggy brows.

"Faster!" he called to the taxi driver in a terse, guttural voice. "A bonus for speed!"

The cab spurted ahead, raced along Northern Boulevard, swung left through the entrance to Holmes Airport.

The swift red and silver Beechcraft cabin biplane was waiting on the line, its propeller already turning.

The Phantom threw a five-dollar bill to the cab driver, lurched out of the taxi, loping in hurrying strides to the plane. The fiery red head of Big Jerry Lannigan, visible through the open window of the cabin's cockpit, turned as Professor Bendix pulled himself into the ship.

"Hiya, Skipper!" Lannigan said, and grinned. "We're going places again, eh? Reminds me of—"

His good-humored voice broke off and the grin on his freckled, weathered face faded abruptly as he recognized the grim determination in the Phantom's darting eyes.

"Get going, Champ," Van then snapped. "Full throttle! We'll talk in the air. Head for Buffalo."

Jerry Lannigan's beefy shoulders hunched over the controls, and the powerful motor roared. The ship taxied rapidly, swung into the wind, thundered down the runway.

A minute later Long Island was dropping swiftly away below them as Jerry wound up the retractable landing gear. The climbing plane banked and headed north across the Sound.

Chapter Five
Hooded Kill

Darkness had descended over the nation's capital. Yet Washington, sweltering in the heat, was a murmuring hive of excitement and near panic. The Rock Canyon Dam disaster was on everyone's tongue.

The lights in the Smithsonian Institute had been turned out, but that building of strange antiques and specimens was being guarded by a Secret Service man.

Standing in a window on the second floor of the Smithsonian Building, Jud Marks, the Federal Bureau of Investigation operative stationed in the building, was staring out at the red marker lights atop the shaft of the Washington Monument. He was a large, rawboned man, with sharp blue eyes, a blond mustache and a jutting jaw.

He turned quickly as a slight shuffling noise caught his ear, but it was only one of the regular night watchmen making his rounds.

Jud Marks signaled the man and turned back to the window. He lighted a cigarette, smoked half of it leisurely, and suddenly dropped it to the floor, scrubbed it out with the toe of his shoe as his narrowed eyes stared down at the driveway below.

A long, black sedan, its headlights extinguished, was rolling to a stop beside the delivery entrance to the building. But nobody got out of the car immediately.

Marks watched the car a moment longer, then moved away from the window toward the stairway. There was, so far as he knew, no official of the Smithsonian Institute who had stayed in the building after it had been closed up for the night, no person here who would have a car call for him.

He started down to investigate, but flattened abruptly against the wall halfway down the staircase as two shadowy figures darted across the corridor below.

Jud Marks jerked out his gun, ran silently the rest of the way down the stairs, following those two fast-moving, furtive figures. He lost them among the glass cases of stuffed reptiles on exhibition in a room of the west wing.

Out in the big dark main foyer an electric flashlight in the hand of one of the regular night watchmen made a thin, yellowish shaft across the stone floor. A second later the light blinked out, clattered onto the flagging, and there was a quick, stifled moan, then the dull thud of a falling body.

Marks ran back into the foyer, his own torch shooting a shaft of light before him.

In the moving beam the watchman's body was a huddled heap on the floor, and a flow of blood coursed redly from a wound in the unconscious guard's back. The protruding black handle of a knife was visible.

This, the tall F.B.I. operative saw in a sliding glance as his torchlight jerked across and outlined for an instant a black-robed, black-hooded figure running through a doorway into the mineral exhibit room.

Marks bent down over the watchman on the floor, saw that he was dead, then plunged after the hooded killer. And as he swung through the open doorway a human catapult hit him.

A knife blade ripped his coat in a swift downward plunge. He whirled aside, slammed into a wall behind him, snapped on his flashlight to get a target for the automatic in his right hand. The light struck full against a corpse-grey mask covering a face hidden beneath a black, monklike hood. The Federal operative's gun fired low, purposely. The robed murderer would be more valuable alive than dead.

But in the split-second it took to change his aim, the grim target spun aside, leaped at him again with poised knife. Marks' slug chipped the stone wall harmlessly.

Then the killer was on him again, cursing with harsh, rasping oaths. The long-bladed knife slashed at Jud, ripped through his sleeve, burned paralyzingly through the flesh of his warding forearm, knocking the electric torch from his grip.

As the light dropped, its rays for a split-second swept down across two more robed and hooded men crouched over an open glass display case. They were lifting from its bed a silver-colored rough ball-like piece of metal the size of a small goldfish bowl-the meteoric fragment Dr. Hugo Junes had taken a chip from.

The torch cracked out against the stone flooring, blotting off the strange tableau. From somewhere off in the darkness another gun exploded and a scream of agony started and broke off. The powerful arms closed around Jud Marks' body, lifting him into the air.

He fought now like a wild man, his gun hand gripped in the viselike fist of his smothering opponent. The man in that weird hooded garb had the strength of a gorilla. Ju jitsu and judo were useless tricks in this swaying, gasping, silent battle.

Marks kicked back with his heels, tried to dislodge the footing of the man holding him off the floor. The grip about his waist only tightened.

He was vaguely aware of blurred movement across in the darkness. A torch gleamed in the doorway at the rear of the room, advanced toward them. The man he was struggling with shrieked out a curse, called for help.

The next moment a second hooded unknown ripped the gun from Marks' grip, cracked him in the jaw with a driving fist. Jud's senses rocked as the second and third blows crashed against him.

"He's not a watchman," an authoritative, icy voice stated. The torch shone blindingly in Marks, eyes. "Who is he?"

"I'll kill him and find out afterward!" The powerful arms took a fresh grip about the F.B.I. man's body.

Jud felt fingers jabbing into his pockets as the light blinked out. He stopped struggling, breathing hard, waiting for an opportunity to break free. He could feel the sharp point of the long knife against his ribs.

"Federal agent of the Bureau of Investigation," the first voice grated as the flashlight jabbed its beam at the badge that had been taken from Marks' vest pocket.

"All the more reason to use the knife on him," the growled voice of the man pinioning Marks' arm said ruthlessly.

"A damned good reason not to!" the man with the electric torch snapped. "Give him the pencil and we'll take him along. We've got what we want here. The chief wants one of these Federals for questioning. Wants to find out how much the bureau knows about him. Use the pencil on him and toss him in the car. We've got to get out of here!"

"I ain't got one of them pencils with me —"

"You're a damn fool!" The hooded, white-masked face in front of Jud Marks came closer, taking a thick black pencil from his pocket.

Marks' slitted eyes glared fearlessly, helplessly.

The hand holding the pencil thrust it close to Jud's face.

"Have a nice nap, copper!"

"I'll see you in hell!" Marks grated defiantly.

"Well-you'll get there eventually yourself," the black-robed man promised.

A cruel, sadistic chuckle sounded behind the Federal agent. A faintly bluish puff of odorless gas squirted suddenly from the pencil into Marks' face. The F. B. I. man gagged, coughed once, then went limp as unconsciousness swept over him.

"Tape him up and lock him in the luggage trunk on the sedan," the one with the electric flashlight directed as he put away his gas pencil. "Everything else is ready. Hurry up. We've got a long hard trip."

The unconscious Secret Service operative was picked up bodily, carried to the delivery entrance, dropped on the floor while adhesive tape was plastered over his eyes and lips and wrapped around his wrists and ankles.

As he was carried out and crammed into the trunk on the rack at the rear of the car, the rough ball of heavy metal the meteoric fragment taken from the glass case in the ore exhibition room, was being wrapped in a blanket and placed in the bottom of the car. Ten minutes later that long, black sedan was purring across the Potomac River into Virginia where it turned to the right and headed north in the night.

Chapter Six
Torture Death

All through the fast two and a half-hour flight against a strong crosswind, Dr. Paul Bendix sat in the front seat beside Lannigan, and seemed half asleep. His cryptic answers to the big red-headed Irishman's questions were enigmatic and curt.

"We'll have to wait, Champ," he told Lannigan flatly, "until we find out what's been going on with Dr. Junes' metallurgical experiments. With murder at one end, and an explosion at the other, there's more than the ordinary crime-for-money motive behind this peculiar affair."

"Some big mob is working again," Jerry declared. "Another gang of crooks like that arson outfit that tried to blackmail New York City, eh? I'd like to get my hands on 'em!"

Van veiled the fragment of a wry smile behind his drooping eyelids. Jerry Lannigan was a whirlwind in a fight, fearless and trustworthy beyond reason, and far from dumb. But it was sometimes a tough job to hold the big fellow back from too sudden action that might warn off the unknown brain operating back of a sequence of crimes.

Jerry Lannigan had been the top sergeant-mechanic in charge of the pursuit squadron that Richard Curtis Van Loan had commanded as a flying major during the World War. And Lannigan, loyal and faithful, kicked and shoved by chance three times around the world since then, had tried to find the man who had been his C.O. in France.

He'd not succeeded, so far as he knew. Four burly but polite doormen had unceremoniously tossed him into the street from the aristocratic entrance to the exclusive London-town Apartments on upper Park Avenue atop which Dick Van Loan had built his penthouse bachelor home. Van Loan owned the building, in fact, but had been away when Lannigan had tried to visit him.

Van had found Jerry by accident, subsequently, during the blowing up of a Bronx River bridge, but had been disguised and Lannigan had not recognized him. Remembering the battling qualities of the big red-headed mechanic. Van had immediately hired him, letting Jerry know only that he was being employed by the Phantom.

It still stood that way now.

For Dick was afraid that Jerry's pride, damaged at having been thrown out of the swanky London-town when Lannigan had tried to look him up, would drive the Champ away if ever the likeable, fiery Irishman found that the one-time flying major he was searching for and the wealthy Park Avenue clubman were the same.

Lannigan knew some of the Phantom's disguises. He would never know the real identity of the man he sought behind those ingenious characterizations.

The Beechcraft's powerful Wasp motor beat a rhythmic, staccato monotone as the late evening sky darkened into night, making conversation difficult. The rain storm of the afternoon had blown north, but the speedy ship outdistanced it. At ten-thirty the glow and flash of Buffalo's lights were under them, and the Phantom swung the control wheel from Lannigan's seat over to his own.

"I'll land at Niagara," he told Jerry. "We'll lock up the ship. You come with me to Dr. Junes' home. I don't know what we'll run into there."

A gleam of anticipation shone in the Champ's greenish eyes as Van cut the throttle and swooped down toward the small unlighted airport at Niagara. Across the dark, thunderous canyon of the mighty falls itself, the glimmering lights of houses and hotels winked mysteriously at them from the Canadian side of the rapids.

A grim reminder of the flood force of the disaster at Rock Canyon Dam seemed to echo through the darkness from the mighty falls as the Phantom set the ship down on the field and snapped off the landing lights.

"What we want," he told Lannigan as they locked up the plane, "is a talk with Junes, if I can get him to talk. He'll know something about Dr. Paul Bendix, because I've managed to get several science articles published in the journals he reads. Then, we want a look at his laboratory, whether he'll take us there or not."

"We've cracked open tougher spots than labs," Jerry reminded him confidently. "We'll get in!"

Ten minutes later Van and Jerry were pulling up in a cab in front of a small, neat cottage on a dark, quiet street at the residence address of the famous metallurgist.

"Just in case," Van whispered to Lannigan, "I couldn't come armed. If I need a rod, how about it?"

"I'm rodded, so don't worry," Jerry told him. "I wouldn't want to answer a phone call from you without a roscoe on my hip."

Several reporters stood on the tree-shrouded sidewalk, talking in low tones with a detective and a uniformed police lieutenant.

"I'm looking for Doctor Junes," the Phantom announced as he got out of the cab. He spoke with a slightly guttural accent, his eyes studying the men and the dark surroundings from beneath the shaggy greying eyebrows of Professor Paul Bendix. "Is the Doctor at home, gentlemen?"

One of the reporters, wearing a ticket in his hat band, eyed the odd, stooped figure in the faded frock coat with interest. "Who are you, Mister?" He added, in a brazen aside to the other men, "This old-timer looks as screwy as Junes himself, eh?"

"I am Professor Paul Bendix!" Van said haughtily. "I am a man of science, so you have doubtless never heard of me!"

The police lieutenant stepped up close. "Didn't you know that Dr. Junes had a nasty explosion in his laboratory early this evening?"

"We just flew up from New York City," Lannigan said gruffly.

The plainclothes detective, watching them suspiciously, glanced at the lieutenant. "If they flew up, they were in the air when the report went out. They wouldn't know, I guess."

The lieutenant nodded, asked bluntly, "What did you want to see Dr. Junes about, Professor Bendix?"

"A purely scientific matter," the Phantom's foreign-accented voice answered curtly. "Doctor Junes is conducting some valuable experiments in metallurgy in which I am interested. My visit here is sponsored by Mr. Frank Havens, the eminent publisher."

"I guess I can tell you, then," the police lieutenant said, his eyebrows going up at mention of the Clarion owner's name. "Dr. Junes had a very mean shock when the explosion happened. Nobody was killed, fortunately. He was brought home by two of his assistants, and refused to talk, except to say that he was finished forever with what he was working on —I don't pretend to understand that part of it, naturally. Anyhow, he suddenly changed his mind about a half hour ago, and went back to the laboratory with the two assistants again."

"If the doctor is at the laboratory, then I should see him there," Van stated. "Is there any reason why not, sir?"

"I suppose you can go there," the officer admitted. "I'll tell you, though, Professor Bendix —a fellow from New York City visited Dr. Junes yesterday, and was murdered in Grand Central Station today when he returned to your city. The New York police notified us, so we are sort of trying to watch out, for the doctor's protection. In fact, we've got a couple of detectives hanging around as close to Dr. Junes as they can get. Which isn't very close, in that lab of his. He's a touchy old codger." The officer studied Dr. Bendix warily.

"What could that have to do with me, sir?" Professor Bendix shrugged, turned toward the cab. "I am concerned with science, not with crime. Thank you for directing me, officer."

He climbed into the taxi with Jerry, ordered the driver to take him to Dr. Junes' laboratory. As the cab pulled away, he turned sideways in the seat, watched narrowly through the rear window.

In the vague darkness behind, he caught a glimpse of the police lieutenant and the two reporters darting across the sidewalk toward Dr. Junes' cottage, evidently intent on using the phone.

"Checking on us," he said quietly to Lannigan. "Perhaps warning the detectives to watch us, or let us go through. We'll soon see."

"If we're going in, we're going in, dick or no dicks," Jerry declared flatly.

Van's eyes clouded, then became sharply alert, determinedly alive again as the taxi stopped in front of a long, squatty low building of bleak stone that stood apart from other dark buildings on a black private lane near the rumbling falls. He got out, paid off the driver, and stood for a minute with Lannigan as the taxi turned and rolled away.

A high iron picket fence surrounded the tree-shaded grounds. The large vehicle gate was locked, but a narrow pedestrian passage beside the empty watchman's booth let them through onto a winding cinder path leading to the dark laboratory.

Van led the way, making no attempt at caution. There was no sign of the detectives the police lieutenant had mentioned.

At the arched main entrance to the squat building he tried the door, found it locked, and rapped resoundingly with his knuckles.

There was no answer for fully two minutes. Then the door opened a few inches and a flash-light gleamed blindingly in their faces.

"Yeah?" a harsh voice demanded suspiciously. "What'd ya want?"

The Phantom ignored the gun visible in the hand of the man with the torch.

"Professor Paul Bendix to see Doctor Hugo Junes," he announced impatiently.

"I'll have to know more than that," the man inside growled.

"Tell the doctor," Van ordered, "that Professor Bendix has arrived from New York City and is to see the doctor in behalf of Mr. Frank Havens, the publisher."

"Wait here." The door shammed shut on them.

"I should have shoved in while he was arguin'," Jerry exclaimed.

Van shook his head. There were other means of getting inside that laboratory, if this direct method failed. If possible, he wanted Dr. Junes to connect Professor Bendix with the murdered Lester Gimble before they met, so the General Electric scientist could be prepared to give him, unobserved, the information Gimble had carried to his death. But he didn't want to use Havens' name unnecessarily.

There was another wait of several minutes before the door opened once more and the torch gleamed at them.

"Come on in," the harsh voice directed.

They shoved into the blackness anteroom. The door shut and the smell of a thousand chemicals assailed their nostrils. Van recognized the predominant odor of fulminated sulphur which increased as they followed the stocky figure who motioned them along with the revolver he held.

Ahead of them the beam of his flashlight outlined the bare walls of a concrete corridor, and steps going down. They descended, their footsteps echoing hollowly.

Another corridor turned off at right angles behind a heavy steel door which the stocky man opened and closed behind them. Van got one good look at his hard features before he padded on ahead again. There was another left turn, a second stairway going down, steeper and longer than the first.

At the bottom they stopped before a massive circular steel vault-like door cut into what appeared to be no longer concrete but solid rock. Their guide could not have come this far and returned during the short few moments they had waited outside the front entrance of the building. He must have phoned down here.

As the man swung open the heavy round door, Van said to him:

"How do you know I'm Professor Bendix?"

The fellow eyed him belligerently. "That'll be up to the doctor. He's down there." The stocky man stood aside, waiting.

Van looked through the circular doorway. A ladder disappeared into the well-like shaft, but light showed at the bottom some twenty feet below as he peered down. Except for a rangy shadow that moved momentarily across the light at the bottom, the hole had every appearance of a death trap.

The Phantom glanced warningly at Jerry Lannigan, nodded swiftly, and stepped onto the steel rungs of the ladder fastened into the circular stone wall. Above him, as he lowered himself, Lannigan's descending bulk blotted out the light of the electric torch above.

A moment later the Phantom stood at the bottom of the hole. He stepped away from the ladder, turned and moved into the queer octagonal laboratory of Dr. Hugo Junes.

One whole side of the laboratory was a wreck. An electric arc oven was blasted apart, and a slab of the rock wall behind it had been blown off. The debris-burnt metal, ore and scorched, blackened stone had been brushed into a heap and partly covered by a collapsed iron screen tipped over it.

The compact but barren-looking equipment across the room that had not been demolished by the explosion was now in use.

Dr. Junes himself-Van recognized the man from his pictures in several of the metallurgical journals he'd studied-was standing tall, gaunt and frightened beside a shelflike high-voltage electric oven which was already glowing whitely beneath the plates covering its heat producing arcs.

Two men, wearing heavy welder's goggles covering their eyes and faces, were watching him alertly, and a third stood back of them at a large rheostat in the wall. He, too, wore similar heavy glasses and face protector.

There was no other equipment in the room except, on a stone slab that made a workbench jutting from the wall opposite the rheostat, a heavy twenty-four-pound sledge hammer, a chisel and a steel handsaw. Beside the hammer was a small chip of silver colored ore the size of a silver dollar.

The tall, gaunt man nearest the furnace looked across at Van with an almost beseeching gleam of hope in his heat-moistened eyes. His gaze shifted a moment to Lannigan, who now stood behind the Phantom, then settled helplessly upon Van again.

"I am told," the unsteady voice of the gaunt, frightened man said with an attempt at formality, "that you are Professor Paul Bendix, of New York City. I believe I have had the pleasure of reading several of your scientific brochures. I am Dr. Hugo Junes."

The Phantom nodded gravely, and his grey eyes veiled their wary alertness beneath the drooping lids of Professor Paul Bendix.

"Excellent, Doctor," he said austerely. "And I am familiar with your remarkable work." He glanced at the glowing furnace. "I observe your experiment is already in process, despite an unfortunate explosion."

"What you observe," Junes stated with suppressed passion, "is the ultimate defeat of all my experiments with aluminum and calbite. I have returned here only to burn up what the attempted fusion reaction did not completely destroy."

The eyes of the others in the room were inscrutable behind their heavy goggles. For the moment, at least, they seemed content to listen and dart quick glances at the furnace.

"I understand your experiments are designed to fuse calbite and aluminum," Van said appreciatively. "But the explosion —"

Dr. Junes' gaze shifted to the others, then to the oven, and back to the Phantom, blinking confusedly. "I have refused to continue, or to leave any trace of my work, because of that revealing accident this afternoon. I am unable to understand what was the real cause of it, sir, but only a few grains of the composite metals, not quite fused, suddenly exploded-with the result you can see for yourself." He waved a hand toward the debris at one side of the room.

"Powerful," Van commented, his nerves tightening as the impact of that information struck him. "A few grains, you say? No more?"

"A very few grains, Professor Bendix. And —" Junes smacked his palms together sharply — "it happened! My assistants do not agree with me in my refusal to continue. But consider-what would happen to humanity if the explosive power of the formula I nearly discovered became a reality! The whole world would be at the mercy of whoever could control that metallurgical combination. It is too dangerous, too terrible to contemplate. So I have refused to go on!"

"It's an endothermic compound, I presume," Professor Bendix suggested, and when Junes nodded agreement, "At what temperature did you expect to make the aluminum-calbite fusion?"

"Impossible to say," Junes declared warmly. "These furnaces produce the greatest heat of any man-made generators yet devised. And they fall considerably short of a real fusion. I've added ammonium nitrate —" He paused, frowned. "But enough. I am done. I will not jeopardize humanity."

The man at the rheostat said sullenly, "Dr. Junes is very stubborn, Professor Bendix. The explosion this afternoon has him imagining too many things a scientist should never consider."

"Bah!" Junes exploded. "You-all of you! I will not be driven, nor forced! Nor bribed. Nor threatened!" His voice rose to a suddenly terrified screech, a pitch that seemed without reason.

Two of the assistants grabbed and held him. The rheostat man nodded curtly, asked Bendix: "Could you, Professor, finish the doctor's experiment-if you were without his hysterical prejudices?"

"Perhaps," Van answered evenly. "Given time."

Dr. Junes' tall figure jerked violently, shuddered, and suddenly collapsed as the two men let him loose. He staggered, stepped backward, his eyes wide with quick terror, staring at the opening behind Van where the steel ladder led up to the sub-cellar corridor above.

The Phantom whirled, knocking against Lannigan's big hand that almost automatically was reaching for a hidden revolver. Van gave Jerry a warning signal to wait. Then Professor Paul Bendix settled his gaze on that exit.

Standing in the well-like opening was a tall, powerfully built figure dressed in a caped black robe with a black hood over a head whose face was masked in white. The next moment the terrifying figure moved into the room.

A frightful scream of agony slashed the silence, shot a blood-chilling shock through Van as he spun back, stared with momentarily paralyzed muscles at the gaunt, writhing form of Junes.

The scientist was sprawled backward halfway across the top of the white-hot furnace plates, his body held there by the adhesive, scorching flesh that stuck to the plates and was filling the room with a nauseating stench. A final shriek died on the doctor's lips. The whole upper half of his body shriveled; the arms alone waving spasmodically in unconscious, dying reflexes.

The Phantom sprang for the rheostat, knocked aside the third masked man standing near it. He spun off the electric dial control, turned to watch the scientist's limp body slide down off the furnace.

For a fleeting second, as one of the men wearing the welding mask bent over Junes' dead body, Van caught a glimpse of the handle of a hypodermic syringe in the fellow's coat pocket. The next moment the handle had slipped down out of sight.

"A regrettable accident," the hooded figure stated sullenly, and glanced at Professor Paul Bendix with icy determination. "Did I hear you say you could carry on the unfortunate scientist's work?"

"This furnace wasn't hot enough for the experiment, anyhow," the masked man who had been at the rheostat declared. "We've been watching this stove seven hours, and the metals won't fuse."

The Phantom's seething mind clicked to a grim conclusion. He was being asked to take the place of the dead scientist. Junes had refused to aid these men in what ever plan they had proposed. Van had not positive proof, but already suspected that the doctor had been shoved onto that furnace and murdered. He decided to join them, let them force him into their scheme.

He nodded, inclined his head gravely, saw even then out of the corner of his eye what was going to happen, as he indicated Lannigan.

"Yes, it is entirely possible that I could conduct the unfortunate doctor's experiment," he said. "If I have my assistant."

At a nod from the hooded figure, one of the men had stepped close to Jerry Lannigan. A faintly blue vapor curled up swiftly from a pencil in the man's hand, and Jerry dropped unconscious to the floor.

"You shall have your assistant," the icy voice promised with a note of satanic humor. He pocketed the small chip of silver-colored ore on the stone bench, and advanced on Van.

The next instant a second pencil ejected a shot of that bluish brain-fogging gas straight into the Phantom's bearded face. The room whirled dizzily for a second that seemed endless, while the hooded face leered. Then oblivion blotted out the room.

Chapter Seven
Destination Darkness

Jolting movement and the sound of rushing wind and an automobile motor's powerful throbbing rhythm beat into the Phantom's drugged brain.

He tried to open his eyes, but the tight pressure of tape on them kept the lids shut. His hands were fastened behind his back with tape. He lurched helplessly with each swerving plunge of the car, his body held upright between two men in the seat beside him.

His parched lips were taped shut, and hunger gnawed at his stomach, giving him the only measure of the passage of time. Eight hours or longer, he judged, since he had been knocked out with those bluish odorless fumes.

The last physical sensations he remembered were the smell of fulmigated sulphur and the heat in that sub-cellar of the General Electric metallurgical laboratory. But now the fresh odor of pines, an occasional lingering whiff of burning coal, and the rush of cool air assailed his senses.

He listened keenly, trying to pick up the rumbling roar of Niagara Falls, but could hear only the hum of the motor and the swish of the wind. The totality of his blind impressions was of steep long climbs, quick descents and open spaces.

The two men sitting beside him began to stir restlessly. A match scraped, followed by the pungent odor of cigarette smoke.

"Making good time for a long ride," one of the men said in a tired voice. "Almost there now. The other car'll be there already."

"Yeah," the other rider agreed. "Not a hitch on this trip. That's what organization does. You going to try for a sergeant's circles?"

"I ain't killed nobody yet," the other grumbled. "Anyhow, not officially. Soon's I do, though, I'll sure apply for the next rating. Sergeant's get plenty of authority."

"You won't have to wait long for a chance to get a killing credit," the second man prophesied knowingly. "I heard, from one of the district majors, that th' State Militia is commin' after us."

"Better not talk too much," the man on Van's right warned. "I heard somethin' about that, too, but you know what the penalty is for not keepin' your mouth shut!"

Van could tell by the movement of the man's body that the guard had gestured significantly at him.

In the prolonged, moody silence that followed, the Phantom tried to fathom the motives and extent of the mysterious organization that three times now had reared its ugly, poisonous head, There was but the one conclusion-some secret society was plotting to overthrow the government of the United States, and was relying upon some new unannounced discovery of modern science to effect their treacherous ends.

And that the dead Dr. Hugo Junes' metallurgical experiments with aluminum and calbite had something to do with those murderous plans appeared obvious. The Phantom was convinced that Dr. Junes' death had not been accidental, but a deliberate killing.

The doctor's pleading fear and final wild hysteria, the hypodermic syringe visible for an instant in one of the masked men's pockets, the whole set-up in the General Electric underground heat laboratory, in fact, pointed at murder. Junes must have been drugged and thrown against the top of that furnace.

But why should these hooded and masked members of such a secret organization kill Dr. Junes, a scientist whom they were using?

The obvious answer was that Junes had refused to conform to their demands. And now the Phantom himself was purposely letting himself be forced to take the murdered scientist's place in their subversive scheme. The disguise of Professor Paul Bendix had proved more real and convincing than Van had ever hoped.

His unanswered and unvoiced questions were interrupted by the slowing of the car. It stopped and, judging by the sounds, they had driven inside some building which, nevertheless, did not smell like a garage. The binding tape was ripped off his ankles and he was shoved out of the car.

His shoes crunched on cinders and there was a trace of coal gas in the air. Then he was being guided along an earthy-smelling, cool passageway that had the confining feel of a tunnel.

There were four men with him now, their rough voices sounding loud and echoing. They stopped him a hundred paces beyond. Van could feel unsteady board footing beneath him.

Something slammed suddenly, sounding like a gate. Mechanism grated and groaned into action. The Phantom, his pinioned arms still held by two of the men, experienced the sensation of being lowered slowly in an elevator.

The complaining, slow descent went on it seemed endlessly. Van had no way of reckoning how far down into the earth he was being carried, but the air became rapidly more gaseous and damp, the pressure heavier.

The guards with him had ceased talking, but their casual, almost illiterate conversation before had given him no inkling of where he might be, except for an occasional miner's phrase.

The elevator car stopped finally and Van was pushed into a narrow passageway. His shoulders rubbed against damp dirt walls, and he had to stoop to protect his head from the low, wooden beams bracing the roof.

From the voices only two men were with him now one in front and one behind. He was herded through an interminably long and crooked tunnel and several times he could feel with his shoulders different openings leading off. Whether or not they were following the main tunnel or any one of its branches, he had no way of knowing.

The floor was a steady decline, some parts steeper than others, but always descending. Five times, the Phantom counted, he was stopped while the exaggerated clicking and grating noise of a door being unlocked, opened, closed behind them and locked again, filled the accentuated silence about him.

The passage leveled out beyond the fifth door. He felt several more openings in the walls as he was shoved ahead. The tunnel twisted continuously, and the odor of gas increased, made breathing more labored.

Another door barred their passage, but there was no key in the possession of the guards for this one. One of them beat against the panel with what sounded like the butt of a gun-five swift blows, a pause and a single sixth.

On the other side a key turned with a click that echoed like an explosion in the compressed atmosphere. A bar scraped as it was slid away from the door on the opposite side. A moment later the door swung inward and the Phantom was pushed through, shoved up against a wall.

He heard the door being closed and locked. Then without preliminaries the tape was ripped off his wrists, torn off his eyes and mouth. Van opened his eyes slowly, slitting them against any unexpected light that might blind him after his long siege of complete darkness. But only a poor indirect glow lighted the cavernous room in which he found himself.

The two men who had brought him in stood on either side of him and one of them held a heavy long-barreled revolver. Both were dressed in overalls and miners' caps in which gleamed small electric bulbs.

Across the chamber stood a tall figure in a black-caped robe. The man had a black hood over his head and his face was covered with a mask through which his eyes glittered ominously. He might have been the same grim specter who had appeared at the General Electric sub-cellar laboratory. Even his voice when he spoke sounded similar in the deceiving echoes of the cavern.

"Professor Paul Bendix," he said contemptuously, "I hope the trip hasn't upset you."

Van eyed the hooded figure defiantly, wet his parched lips. "What manner of science is it," he demanded in the guttural voice of Professor Bendix, "that makes such humiliating experience necessary?"

The hooded man shrugged indifferently beneath his robe.

"Asking questions is not a part of your job here," the tall man stated flatly, and added significantly, "You witnessed what happened to your predecessor, Dr. Hugo Junes."

The Phantom stepped away from the wall, flexing his cramped muscles. In another corner of the cavern his eyes, accustomed to the peculiar light now, slid and settled on the bound and gagged figure of Jerry Lannigan. The big Irishman was watching him eagerly.

"You have my assistant here, I see!" the Phantom exclaimed, making his words ring with anger that covered the relief he felt. "Untie him!" This was no time for feeling his way. They evidently still thought he was an eminent scientist, and he had to continue his bluffing characterization.

"I had your assistant untied before," the cloaked leader in the room said. "He became unmanageable and fought, so I had him tied again to keep him from getting hurt. I hope that the fool will behave himself now that you are here."

"I'll guarantee that he will," Professor Bendix declared gravely. Yet within him was a warming glow at the thought of what damage the Champ had probably done before they overpowered him.

The hooded leader nodded to one of the guards, who went over and ripped the tape bonds from Lannigan's ankles, wrists and lips. The red-headed Irishman got to his feet, came over and stood belligerently beside the professor.

"This joint is ratty!" Lannigan growled at the man in the hood, and turned to Van. "The whole place is overrun with these guys dressed up like Ku Kluxers."

"Enough of that!" the leader snapped. "You'll find our organization very effective if you try any foolishness."

"Quiet," the Phantom warned Lannigan, and addressed the man in the black robe: "If I am to be put to work, I must see the laboratory. And I would appreciate knowing where I am."

The tall, hooded figure again jerked his head at the two mine guards and moved to another door in the chamber.

"You will find where you are," he said over his shoulder, "when the time comes and you are a blood member with us. For the present, the temporary laboratory is directly under us."

The two guards, both of them with guns in their hands now, motioned Van and Lannigan to follow their leader. Van, while he had been talking, had been using his hands casually, feeling of his clothes and secret pockets. His captors appeared not to have taken time to search him thoroughly.

Even though unarmed, he and the Champ might have put up a fight in an attempt to break free. But the information he wanted was evidently down here, not elsewhere.

Escape now would have defeated his purpose.

Guarded by the two armed men, Van and Jerry followed the robed figure through the door which he opened, down a steep incline that turned twice at right angles and brought them out into a deeper, smaller cavern cut into the earth directly below the subterranean chamber above.

Heat greeted them as they entered this room.

Four burly men, stripped to the waist, eyed them curiously. A fifth man who appeared to be a hunchback looked up leeringly with small pale eyes set deep and wide apart in a distorted, twitching and scarred face.

But it was the glow in the center of the room that held Van's attention. Through a small opening in the rock a thin flame stood up from the floor for almost a foot in height. The rock from which this jet spurted was white hot, and the flame itself was perfectly colorless at the base but flowered into vivid blues and yellows before it expended itself.

The room was filled with a constant hissing sound, a miniature roar that made speech difficult.

The Phantom tore his eyes from that fascinating light, and for a moment as he looked away he was blinded. Then vision returned swiftly, but he kept his eyes off that flame, and noticed that about the necks of the four workmen and the hunchback hung thick goggles.

The cloaked leader indicated the short squat man with the hunched back, and said to Van, "This is Doctor Kag. Professor Kag was one of the foremost metallurgists in the world until one of his experiments blew up and crippled him. He is temporarily —" He emphasized the word forebodingly —"in charge of the experiments we are conducting here. The gas flame in this room, with the addition of oxygen, is the hottest torch that has ever been discovered-two thousand degrees centigrade higher than that electric arc oven of Dr. Junes at Niagara Falls."

The Phantom's eyes showed a sharpened interest that he did not have to fake.

The man-made oven of Dr. Junes, built by the General Electric Company for experimental purposes, had the highest temperature of any arc furnace thus far designed. And arc furnaces were the hottest known to man.

Yet, by the statement of one of the engineers in this hooded organization, seven hours of that arc heat had failed to fuse the two metals whose union had been the aim of Doctor Junes. Van did not doubt the statement of the leader standing before him now. And two thousand more degrees of heat, he realized, would be more than sufficient, if properly controlled, to effect that world-important fusion of those two metals.

He was about to speak, when Kag came swaying toward him, leering, pawing with gnarled, crippled hands.

"Professor Junes!" Kag's voice was shrill, piercing.

"He's not Junes," the hooded man shouted. "He's another scientist. Junes is dead, burned up in his own furnace!"

Kag's pale eyes rolled wildly in their sockets. "You're not Junes?" he cried querulously.

"No," Van admitted, watching the man narrowly. There was near insanity in those crazy, rolling eyes.

Suddenly the hunchback's fawning attitude changed. Crazed genius glittered in his rocking gaze.

"Ach!" he screamed. "A scientist, are you? It is I who am the scientist-the greatest scientist in the world! What do you know of science-of fire-of metallurgy?"

"I was a friend and contemporary worker with Dr. Junes," Van answered as calmly as he could. This hunchback, he knew, could trip him with questions, show him up as an impostor. "Tell me, Professor Kag, what experiments you are working —"

"Kag!" The hunchback's shrill voice trembled with frenzy. "Kag! I shall tell you nothing! I shall ask you questions! You do not even know who I am. Kag!"

The Phantom saw the mistake he had made, tried to stop the man's wild screeching by correcting the error. This man was unquestionably Dr. Gulliver Vonderkag, once the foremost metallurgical scientist in Germany-but now only the shell of him, yet his genius still raged.

But Van could not make himself heard.

"A metallurgist, are you? Tell me quickly the fusion point of antimony and copper."

The Phantom's muscles tensed at the suddenness of this crisis.

"Antimony and copper —"

Van had to hesitate, grope an instant before the answer came to him. Then he gave it, watching the hunchback nervously. If the German scientist shot many more such questions at him, he'd be stuck, and his Bendix role unmasked.

"Slow," Kag cried in disgust. "Dr. Junes, he would have been quicker. I could have used him in my work. But you —"

"You've no choice in the matter, Kag," the hooded leader said flatly. "Test him again."

The Phantom's mind fought against Vonderkag's warped brain, beat the crippled scientist's formulating question by sheer audacity and drive.

"Doctor!" Van shouted. "Let us stop this kindergarten child's game. I am interested only in your knowledge of Dr. Junes' work-his experiment which he refused to continue."

"Refused to continue?" Kag demanded shrilly. "What is that?"

"Fusing aluminum and calbite," the Phantom declared in a loud, challenging voice. "Dr. Junes, as you've been told, was killed, but before he died, he had refused to carry on the fusion. He was afraid. I know what he feared. Do you?"

"Afraid?" Kag screeched the word as though it had come from a foreign tongue and had no meaning for him. "Are we men of science?"

Somebody pounded on the door. The hooded leader swung round, unlocked the door, let in a man dressed similarly in hood and robe but without a mask. On the sleeve of the newcomer was a green circle with a zigzag line running through it.

"What's the trouble, Sergeant?" the masked man demanded.

The hooded sergeant saluted briskly, swinging his arm in toward his stomach and out again. He stepped around a water pail, his leg brushing the dipper sticking out of it as he handed over a sealed envelope.

"Something that demands immediate attention," he stated.

As the man in the mask ripped open the envelope and extracted the folded sheet of note paper it contained, Van signaled Lannigan to be ready, and edged closer to the leader whose eyes narrowed dangerously as he read the penciled notation.

For a swift instant, Van caught a glimpse of that note, got a flash view of the words:

Professor Bendix suspected of being sent as a scientist spy from the capitalist publisher —

He managed to catch the name Havens in the note. As he moved, Van remembered he'd used Havens' name in Niagara Falls. The invisible organization had caught up with him!

But what he did now he had already planned to do in that continued moment of suspense when Vonderkag had challenged him as a metallurgical scientist. The crisis demanded instant action; Kag was forgotten for the instant.

With one quick swing, so swift as to be almost undetectable, Van's right arm shot out and downward as his hand gripped the water pail, lifted it, swung its contents straight into the hissing gas flame in the center of the floor.

Instantly the entire room became a dense fog of swirling, blinding steam. The Phantom whirled, and his fist cracked against the jaw of the nearest mine guard. He yanked the gun from the falling man's hand, heard the harder crack of Lannigan's hamlike fist as Jerry slugged the other guard.

"Out!" Van barked.

The next second he was through the door with Jerry puffing behind him. Back of them in the furnace chamber, shouts and shots sounded as slugs pounded into the wall after them.

Chapter Eight
Lannigan's Trick

Near the first turn in the inclined passageway, the Phantom stopped to make sure Lannigan was still coming. The big Irishman plunged past, carrying something heavy over his shoulder.

They raced on up, lunged into the larger cavern above. The place was empty.

Van slammed the door shut, slid down an iron crossbar, locking it. He jerked out his pencil flashlight that the guards had not taken away from him. In its thin shaft he saw Lannigan dumping the hooded figure of the sergeant on the floor.

"How long can we hold them off?" the Irishman demanded. "I brought this guy along so that you could use his costume."

"Not very long, Champ," the Phantom said tersely. "They'll shoot the door off its hinges." He looked quickly at the sergeant. The unmasked face was ordinary, unintelligent. "Get into those robes yourself," the Phantom directed. "One of us has got to get out of this mine and get to Havens. You're elected." He bent down over the unconscious man, began unfastening the black hood.

Shots began crashing into the barred door as Van handed up the costume to Lannigan.

"I'd rather stay here and let you go up, Phantom," Jerry growled as he shrugged into the black outfit.

"I've got to stay. Got to find out more about this organization and the metal they're fusing with that heat," Van insisted. "You get to Havens and fly back here. He'll know what to do when you tell him what's happening. Come on!"

Van's light guided them through the door through which they had first come. Behind them, the barred entrance to the passageway below was trembling on its hinges under the onslaught of the hooded leader and Kag and the hunchback's four burly helpers.

With Lannigan running ahead in the disguise of the sergeant they ran swiftly along the level tunnel toward the first guarded gate. Suddenly, Lannigan ducked into one of the side passages as a bobbing electric headlight on the cap of someone approaching gleamed in the darkness ahead.

Van slid in beside Jerry. The racket of shots and shouts back along the passageway echoed and re-echoed against the walls.

"That's the guard at the next doorway," Van warned. "You've got the black uniform, Champ. Go get him!"

Lannigan's grunt of satisfaction was eager. He took Van's pencil flashlight, stepped out in the path of the advancing guard.

"What's going on down there?" the man shouted excitedly.

The torch in Lannigan's hand gleamed, caught the guard full in the face, outlining his hood and robe and the revolver in his fist.

He jerked to a halt, stopped by the blinding glare of the flash. Jerry gave him no chance to ask anything more. The big Irishman's hammerlike knuckles hit the guard's jaw. The fellow seemed to bounce up off the floor of the tunnel, hang suspended in the air an instant before he dropped back and lay still.

The Phantom darted out, snaked the black costume off the man's body, got into it himself. He took the man's gun, ran on again, urging Lannigan ahead of him.

They were both outfitted in organization uniforms now, and both had two guns apiece. But there was a maze of black, guarded passageways and doors ahead of them, and they had still no identification or countersigns to get them through.

A powerful flashlight sent its beam into the tunnel behind them as the imprisoned men broke loose from the cavern. The Phantom and the Champ raced through the now unguarded first gate into the upgrade underground passage ahead. There was no way of locking those doorways on the entrance side, for only the guards on the inside of the tunnel openings could bar them.

"Take the first turn to the left that looks like something!" The Phantom directed. "We can't take time to lay out every door guard we come to."

A moment later, as the light grew larger behind them, they whirled off the main corridor into a side passage that led up sharply. As he ran, the Phantom tugged off the tell-tale Van Dyke of Professor Paul Bendix. That character was done now, so far as this mysterious subterranean organization was concerned. He thrust the beard up into a crevice between the wall and a wooden tunnel brace, and caught up with Lannigan again.

The passage broke unexpectedly into a large cavern along one wall of which cement sacks were stacked to the roof. In the opposite wall was a large steel door built into a heavy concrete and stone abutment. The door was locked with several large handles and two wheels that gave it the appearance of a steel vault. The construction was recent. Van recognized it as a watertight compartment lock, built to hold back one of the subterranean lakes found in all deep mines. This lower level series of shafts and channels under the operating portion of the coal mine had evidently been used and abandoned, for there was no sign of recent operation this far down and they had come upon no workmen.

There were three exits from this cave, one of them unmarked, the other two marked respectively in chalk on their frame braces: SHAFT 9 and CAGE.

"Which way, Skipper?" Jerry asked.

The Phantom stopped running, glanced back and listened. For a moment there was no sound of pursuit.

"The cage," Van answered, and led the way. "We'll probably run into someone. Don't shoot if you can use your fists."

They advanced more cautiously, and as they went forward along the slightly rising tunnel, Van manipulated some of the make-up of Dr. Bendix that remained on and inside his face.

His nose became more normal as he removed the two small aluminum pieces that had given it the broadened, heavy appearance. The injection of the specially prepared compound that he had shot into his cheeks and jowls had already been partially absorbed and dissipated. He ordinarily had to renew his make-up for any disguise every twenty-four hours. It was, he realized, only the dumbness of his captors and the demand for speed on the part of their leaders, that had made them forego the opportunity they had had to strip him while he had been unconscious.

Even so, it required the expert, trained eye of a physician to detect the fact that one of his complete characterizations was a fraud. By the time he and Jerry had gone another two hundred yards through the shaft, the face of Professor Paul Bendix had completely disappeared, although beneath the black robe Van wore, the frock coat was still a dangerous piece of evidence.

"If this tunnel don't end pretty soon," Jerry panted behind him, "we don't need any elevator. We'll have walked out of here!"

"Just so we get you free of this place, Champ," Van replied.

A half minute later a voice challenged them from somewhere ahead, and another voice, harsher than the first, repeated the warning.

"Keep going," the Phantom whispered to Lannigan, and answered the challenge with a terse, "Show your light, you fools!"

A strong torch beam caught them immediately in a blinding glare. Van stopped, tried to look beneath that light.

"Password!" the harsh voice demanded.

The Phantom's eyes glinted. "Two suspected men have escaped from Professor Kag's shaft!" he snapped, ignoring the password demand. "If they haven't got this far, send word ahead!"

"Whose orders?" the first voice asked sharply from the intense blackness behind the flash-light's unswerving beam.

"Sergeant Flannigan is with me," Van said angrily. He glanced over his shoulder. "Sergeant —"

Jerry stepped to the front, glowering, showing the gun in his hand. His rough voice bellowed: "Who th' hell is giving orders here?"

"I am!" the harder voice snapped, and a tall, hooded and masked man stepped partway into view. On his robed sleeve was the green circle with two crossed yellow zigzagged markers through it. "I'm Commander Rotz!"

The authority in his voice was unmistakable. Van tensed, and gave the peculiar salute he had observed back in Kag's cavern. Lannigan, too, saluted uncertainly.

And at the same instant, the Phantom's keen ears heard the first faint sounds of the pursuit far back along the tunnel.

They were trapped!

Commander Rotz heard that growing sound of voices footsteps also, for he suddenly whipped up his gun, covering them menacingly.

"Stand where you are!" he ordered grimly. "I've seen deserters try to get away like this before."

The Phantom's left hand jerked abruptly at Jerry Lannigan's stolen black robe, a hard, unexpected tug that yanked the beefy Irishman off balance. If Lannigan had made that quick movement himself, some slight flick of warning would have given him away. But Van's quickness had precluded that.

In the split-second that the commander with the leveled gun took to correct his aim, the Phantom's right foot kicked up, hit the masked man's hand at the wrist behind the revolver.

A sharp cry of pain broke from the fellow's hidden lips. The gun spun from his fingers. And Van's fist exploded against the man's jaw!

In the sudden violent confusion, the light fell to the floor of the shaft as Jerry leaped at the other guard. For a matter of seconds there was only gasping, strangled breathing. Then the muffled sound of quick movement and the rustle of cloth.

It was less than a full minute, all told, when Van's fingers found the powerful torch on the dirt floor and snapped it on briefly. In its bright light, Lannigan was bent over the dead figure of the guard, his big hands going through the fellow's clothing.

And the Phantom was standing erect in the black robe, hood and white mask of Commander Rotz. The lifeless, frock-coated body of a man who might have been, beneath his masked features, Professor Paul Bendix, lay at his feet.

Even Lannigan stared twice at the swift, complete transformation before he recognized the Phantom's voice ordering him to action.

"Drag that guard out of sight somewhere," Van directed tensely. "Dump him some place where he won't be found immediately. Get on ahead of me and if you get a chance to get out of here, take it!"

"Okay, Skipper! That's the fastest make-up change I've ever seen you put on." Lannigan grabbed up the dead guard as the light in Van's hand turned toward the sloping end of the shaft up which they had come. The glare of the torch completely hid Jerry's movements behind it as he carried his burden further up the tunnel.

The Phantom kept his light on, faced the pursuers who were already shouting to him above the hard, echoing pounding of their feet. Behind the white mask, his lips were a thin, determined line.

"Halt!" he shouted above the increasing clamor. "Password!"

His voice was harsh and sharp now, like the voice of Rotz. He recognized in the beam of the electric torch the foremost of the advancing crew-one of the mine guards who had been with him in Kag's cavern. The others were strange faces, men picked up in the search that had split into several parties.

"September Third!" the guard snapped back at him and saluted.

September Third! There was grim significance in that countersign.

Van pointed his light down at the figure on the tunnel floor. "You're hunting for that?" he demanded harshly.

The guard and the others with him stared. The identity of the dead Rotz would eventually be discovered, but for the moment the resemblance to Bendix was close enough to fool them. The guard nodded, glanced up.

"There was another one —a big, heavy man with red hair."

"Didn't come this way," Van stated with a ring of authority his voice. "This man was sneaking along here and refused to stop when I challenged him. I've sent the guard stationed here to report this in Shaft Nine. Take your men and come with me. I'll send you up to report on top."

He turned, started up the inclined tunnel in the direction Jerry had taken. There was a sharp curve in the shaft that ended fifty yards beyond at a rough gate that barred the entrance to an elevator car.

There was no sign of Lannigan. The Phantom breathed easier.

"This car shouldn't be left down here now, with a deserter loose. Take it up," he ordered.

"The fellow wasn't a deserter," the guard leading the others told him. "He was a spy —"

"He'll be a dead spy if we catch him," Van promised. "Now get going with that car and report topside!"

The guard saluted again, got onto the car with the three men who had come with him. The elevator trembled in its loose, rough framework as it started to move upward.

The Phantom's light was on it, watching. Where in hell was Lannigan? —The question was answered a second later. Only the protection of the white mask he wore kept back the jolt of sheer shocked surprise that twisted Van's features; He stared, almost unbelieving.

Jerry Lannigan's beefy bulk was hanging beneath the rising floor of the shaft cage, his ham-like hands gripping the cross-bracing under the car! The Champ let go with one hand, waved to Van, and pointed down under him.

The Phantom understood. Lannigan had dumped the body of the dead guard into the elevator well. There was no need even to look.

Van switched off the electric torch, stood in complete darkness.

Chapter Nine
Find the Imperator!

Half a second later he was running noiselessly back along the narrow tunnel. Jerry might be able to get through up above. If audacity and courage counted, Van was confident he would. But there was more information needed about this subterranean organization down here, before any outside help would be of value. Without more knowledge than he had, a raid would only drive the members of this mysterious society of revolt deeper into their hidden holes. Somewhere there was a leader, a single brain, governing and directing this mob-mad legion of doom. Not until that leader was ferreted out could this terror-inspiring organization be broken up and destroyed.

The Phantom decided upon a bold stroke. He had got rid of the clothes of Dr. Paul Bendix, wore now the complete equipment of the dead Commander Rotz.

And he had the password-September Third!

He retraced the path up which he and Jerry had fled from Kag's cavern. In his stolen commander's uniform there was no difficulty in getting by the reguarded barriers he and Jerry had fought through before.

He went directly to Kag's cavern. The hunchbacked scientist was still there, with two of his stripped helpers, and two hooded but unmasked guards whom Van had not seen before, but who eyed him with considerable respect.

"I understand there's been some trouble down here," the Phantom rasped in the voice of Commander Rotz as he entered.

The men, excepting Kag, saluted him with that same peculiar and suggestive movement of the clenched fist across the stomach.

"A dangerous scientist sent to spy on us for the capitalists," Kag exclaimed with renewed excitement, and gave a garbled account of Professor Bendix and his beefy assistant who had been caught and escaped. "An ignoramus!"

As he talked, the crippled scientist unfastened a blanket from a heavy, round object on the floor, began stroking the rough, silver-colored ball of metal.

"What's that?" Van demanded, keeping his eyes off the white jet of flame shooting up through the center of the floor, but motioning at the ball with his hand.

"Ach!" Kag's wild eyes rolled and glistened. "A meteoric fragment!" he exclaimed. "From the Smithsonian Institute. It was the only proof in the world that aluminum and calbite could be fused-but the world lacks that proof now. The Imperator and I alone hold this secret. Not even the famous Dr. Junes could do what I have done!"

"I've heard about it," the Phantom said. "And you too, Dr. Vonderkag."

The hunchbacked German expert in metallurgy smiled at the mention of his real name, and grew more voluble.

"You are interested, I see," he cried. "I will tell you —I have fused calbite and aluminum in that flame there, and have made the lightest, toughest metal ever conceived by man! Soon, we plan to manufacture this for our own purposes, in quantity!"

Kag's statement ended in a series of shrieks and idiotic chuckles of secret merriment. Van wanted to ask him more, but at that moment another sergeant entered, stared round and saluted him, handing over a note. The Phantom accepted the piece of paper, read the order printed in pencil:

IMPERIAL BOARD STAFF MEETING
IMMEDIATELY IN THE SHAFT 9
BARRACKS. KINDLY ATTEND.

THE IMPERATOR.

Van stared at the order through narrowed eyes, his every nerve alert and tingling. He nodded at the sergeant, shoved the paper into a pocket under his black robe.

"I shall call upon you again, Professor Vonderkag," he said, and strode out.

As he went back up the incline and out into the main corridor, he noticed with surprise that the passageway was now heavily guarded, with sentries stationed every thirty or forty yards. Each of them threw their electric torches upon him and saluted him as he passed.

Several other men were standing along some distance ahead, receiving the same crisp salutations as himself. It didn't seem possible that he was soon to meet the Imperator in person. Yet the Imperator's name was the authority on that order in his pocket.

He passed through the cavern where the steel water door was set in the concrete, followed the two men ahead of him into the underground corridor marked SHAFT 9. The tunnel curved to the left away from the passage that led to the elevator cage up which Lannigan, he hoped, had made his escape.

Two guards at a heavy wooden door took up his written order, passed him on into an extraordinarily large and long chamber of cavernous height. The place, lighted by lanterns that threw grotesque shadows along the walls, was already a scene of weird assembly.

All of the men present were robed, hooded and masked. Each of them wore upon his sleeve a green circle of the clan. And through each circle ran the double zigzag emblem that marked them as ranking officers.

There was no fraternizing. The men did not gather in the usual small groups while they waited. Each man stood aloof from his companions, as though afraid of being caught discussing their mutual organization affairs.

The Phantom moved over against a wall, looking about eagerly for some centralizing nucleus to this strange silent gathering, There was no dais, no raised platform.

Suddenly, without preliminaries, an incisive, chilling and metallic voice filled the cavern-the same voice that had come over the air to announce the Rock Creek Dam disaster sixty seconds before it happened.

Van's darting eyes slid over the room, searching for the source of that metallic flow of words. Of the fifty men present, not a lip moved. Yet the voice went on:

> "Attention, officers of the Invisible Empire! Rock Canyon Dam has been successfully destroyed! Not a clue that could be traced to us was left. And only ten of our men were obliged to sacrifice their lives to protect our Order. Their families, according to our constitution, will be financially independent now for seven generations."

Van's eyes glittered behind his white mask as the full significance of that statement struck him. With such a guarantee of financial security as a reward for sacrifices to this carefully schemed out organization, there was practically no limit to the hysterical courage which such a bait engendered.

The cold, inhuman voice went on: "Our next attack upon the government will occur at dawn on September 3rd. I myself, at that hour four days hence, will bomb the United States Treasury Building at Washington, using the airplane that has been built of the aluminum-calbite metal being manufactured here. A new explosive, more powerful than the explosive used at Rock Canyon, will be dropped from my plane. I shall detail a detachment to carry here the United States Treasury gold."

Throughout the cavern there was a sharp intake of greedy breath as this announcement was made. But the invisible speaker continued emotionlessly:

> "One other matter at this time. Through our intelligence service I have been warned that a capitalist scientist, Dr. Bendix, has attempted to gain admittance to our headquarters here. It is suspected that Mr. Frank Havens, an enemy publisher, has employed this man.

"A Professor Bendix and an assistant did appear here. I have two reports, neither of them checked sufficiently. One is that these two men escaped. The other is that one of them, presumably Bendix has been killed. I shall send at once a man disguised as Doctor Bendix to visit Mr. Havens in New York. This envoy will remove the publisher. I call for a volunteer."

Instantly, the Phantom's hand was raised in the air and his voice rang out:

"I, Commander Rotz, offer myself for that honor!"

There was an imperceptible silence while the eyes of every officer in the room turned toward him. Then the chilling voice of the unseen speaker again:

"Commander Rotz is accepted. He will advance at once, at the conclusion of this meeting, along the unnumbered gallery next to Shaft 9. He will be met. That is all, gentlemen. I, the Imperator, have spoken!"

The Phantom's pulse pounded wildly. He out-stared the eyes watching him, turned quickly and strode out of the barrack cavern, the Imperator's icy words ringing in his ears:
"Advance along the unnumbered gallery."
He would be met.

Chapter Ten
Horror Cave

Van was gripped by the first real hope of unmasking the power-mad genius behind the Invisible Empire. It quickened his senses, keyed him to alertness.

Not once since he had tricked his way into this maze of subterranean passageways had he been able even to guess at the position of the headquarters of the organization. It would have been impossible to track out the black, labyrinthian corridors of this vast series of connected mines and expect to stumble upon the center of the hooded society.

Nor had he heard anyone except Kag mention so much as the existence of a leader. He suspected none of the robed members or the guards had ever seen the Imperator face to face. There seemed to be some unwritten law against speaking his name.

That was the most baffling phase of this strange underground hunt-the utter and impregnable silence of the members.

The Phantom had considered Vonderkag as a suspect, but the hunchback scientist seemed too excitable, too unstable to govern such a ruthless association of men. Yet, apart from Kag, who was there, of all those masked and hooded members, that he could challenge as being the Imperator? A single such open attempt would only end in his immediate death.

The fifty masked officers who had attended that cryptic meeting in the cavern barrack were automatically eliminated as ultimate Imperator suspects, for that cold, emotionless speech had been delivered from some point outside that underground chamber.

Van had thought of trying to escape from this subterranean warren, to contact Havens and get help. He'd have to get out and warn the publisher, after this last threat. But to have these tunnels surrounded by police or soldiers would be useless. The Invisible Empire would only fade deeper into the mines and emerge at will from a hundred different exits.

He was stopped by two guards at the entrance to the tunnel leading off from the cavern that had the concrete walled water door of steel. They let him through at mention of the name Commander Rotz.

He went on alone, his flashlight outlining the earth walls of the sharply rising passage.

The tunnel curved several times, and ended at an iron door that was unlocked. He swung it open, found that it was the entrance to an elevator. The car was empty.

Van stepped into the cage, closed the iron door, and tried the operating lever. The elevator would not lower, but it went up rapidly when he reversed the control.

So far as he could determine, there were no stage landings until the car stopped of its own accord. He opened the door again, stepped out into a short corridor.

Two more guards in robes, masks and hoods, stood before the only exit, a narrow steel door set in a wall of cement at the end of the passage. There was an electric battery lamp over their heads.

The Phantom advanced, gave his name again. A key jangled in the lock, and the door swung open for him. He stepped through the opening into a lighted room of solid white concrete, heard the door close and the lock click behind him.

An odor of disinfectant and medicine permeated the place which was a combination surgical ward and operating room. Against one wall was a glass cabinet holding several trays filled with delicate, razor-sharp instruments. Beyond it was another door opposite the one he had entered, closed and evidently locked from the other side.

In the center of the room stood two operating tables, with space to work between them.

Van's eyes slid around the place, and a low moan sounded behind him. He turned, stepped behind a screen, looked down at a cot. On that stiff bed lay a man whose face was scarcely recognizable as human!

Van gazed pityingly into the agonized eyes of the helpless patient, and drew in his breath sharply. The skin on that mutilated face had been removed from more than two-thirds of its area. The cheeks, jowls, jaw and nose were raw flesh, and both ears had been amputated. The pillow upon which the head rested was bloodstained, sticky with gore.

The man's eyes clung to the Phantom's masked face wildly, then roved to the bed stand at the head of the cot. Van followed that tortured glance, and started at what he saw.

On the enameled top of the stand lay a gold badge and an identification card. He picked them up, his own eyes narrowing as he read the name:

JUD MARKS
Federal Bureau of Investigation

Van's hand shoved back the black hood he wore, and jerked off his white mask. He reached beneath his black robe and his fingers dug into a pocket in the belt he wore under his clothes.

Then he bent over the man on the bed, and held before the Secret Service operative's eyes a small, flat platinum badge studded with bright diamonds set in the shape of a mask-the Phantom's seal. Few men had ever seen that badge, but its legend was a by-word of accomplishment in police circles, an emblem of terror among criminals.

The eyes of the tortured F.B.I. man became alive with recognition and hope as he stared at the diamond mask in Van's hand. He tried to nod, and his bloody lips formed the word "Phantom!"

Dick Van Loan replaced the badge in his belt, bent again over the man on the bed.

"Can you talk?" he asked eagerly. "Who brought you here?"

The G-man's mangled face shuddered with the effort to answer. His words came slowly, painfully weak:

> "An attempt had been made to rob Smithsonian Institute —I was-guarding it-Hoods-like yours" —his agonized glance roved over Van's black costume — "jumped me-stealing a —meteor from-ore case. Been trying to make-me talk about the Bureau-since I woke up here —"

Van's eyes gleamed. That meteoric fragment he'd seen and that Kag had boasted about down in the furnace cavern-it had come from the Smithsonian Institute. Kag had gloated over its theft.

"Who did this to you-here?" he urged.

"A doctor-big man-couldn't see his face —I'm dying."

The F.B.I. man's hand moved beneath the thin, stained sheet.

Van pulled back the bloody covering, saw that Jud Marks was shackled to the bed. More skin had been cut from his arms, chest and stomach. The G-Man's fingers gestured-desperately.

The Phantom gripped that bony hand, held it warmly, while his narrowed gaze clung to Marks' glazing eyes. The man was dying, and knew it.

Van swallowed back the burning, hard lump choking in his throat. This was death, ruthless, horrible, yet a blessed relief for Jud Marks from the torture of unceasing pain.

The G-man's fingers in the Phantoms' hand slowly relaxed. The Federal agent's eyes became glassy, vacant, staring sightlessly.

Van lowered the limp hand to the bed, pulled the sheet up over the dead man's ghastly face. Gravely, a bleak look of intense determination growing in his eyes, he picked up and pocketed Jud Marks' badge and identification.

If Van escaped from here alive, those two grim articles would be returned to the Federal Bureau of Investigation at Washington. And the name of Jud Marks, G-Man, would appear on the engraved honor roll there, another hallowed addition to that heroic record of courageous warriors who had lost against crime.

As he stood there moodily, his thoughts still on the murdered Federal investigator, the Phantom's fingers toyed nervously with a physician's thermometer on the bed stand. He shook himself out of his brief, grisly reverie, glanced about the room, preparatory to giving it a quick search. His eyes shifted back to the thermometer in his hand.

He held it closer, looking for the manufacturer's stamp. And suddenly an eager gleam leaped into his narrowed grey gaze.

Printed on that sliver of glass, the two words partially rubbed away by use, was the ownership legend:

Alleghany Penitentiary.

As he stared at that name, Van's mind leaped back to Frank Havens' office in the Clarion Tower, and the tableau of death that had been enacted there.

The picture was startlingly vivid-the murdered metallurgical expert, Lester Gimble, lifeless in the armchair beside Havens' desk; the two homicide detectives with Captain Walters; Havens himself; and the three officials from the Alleghany Prison.

Warden Jack Bluebold; Dr. Maurice Jessup, the resident physician: ex-Congressman Harry Arnold, Chairman of the Board of Pardons and Parole. Van hadn't forgotten them.

Even at that time, it had struck him as odd that they should have been sitting in the Clarion publisher's private office at the precise moment when an escaped lifer from the Alleghany stir was identified as the dead murderer of the metallurgical specialist employed by Havens.

The Phantom stepped resolutely across to the instrument tray between the two grim operating tables, took from it the metal container for the thermometer that someone had left there. He thrust the thermometer in its cover, put the case in his pocket.

That slim glass tube of mercury would be used as evidence, if the time ever came when the facial surgeon and skin grafter was caught. And he should be here now, if the Imperator still meant to disguise Commander Rotz and send him as Professor Paul Bendix on the murderous mission to Havens.

Van glanced at those fine, sharp knives and instruments in the glass cabinet against the wall! The Imperator's genius for evil went beyond any make-up table, and resorted to surgery that cut any moulded living flesh to suit its deadly purposes.

Grimly, the Phantom decided to see it through, despite his discovery of the thermometer clue and his realization that he himself would be recognized as Dr. Bendix again. It was an immediate chance to meet the surgeon, probably the Imperator himself. He pulled the ghost-white mask back up over his face, tugged the black hood down over his head.

The two revolvers he had appropriated with Jerry Lannigan down there deeper in the mine warrens felt good in his belt under the black robe.

And suddenly he heard harsh, clipped voices outside in the short corridor where the two masked guards kept watch. Judging by the different tones that came through the steel door, five or six more men had just come up in the elevator and joined them.

The Phantom crouched at the door, listening. Some of the words out there came through distinctly:

"—found Commander Rotz dead down below —"

"What're the orders? Do we wait?"

"Open up! Imperator's instruction-He won't be here now. Get in there and kill the spy —"
The voices lowered to whispered directions.

Van's nerves steadied under the desperate change in the situation. He realized clearly what had happened. The Imperator had already discovered that the dead man wearing the clothes of Professor Paul Bendix was not Bendix at all but Commander Rotz himself.

Eventually, that discovery had to be made, and the Phantom's quick change of disguises shown up. Van had hoped it would not happen so fast, but now that it had-He darted across the room, tried the opposite door, but found it was too securely barred on the other side.

Out in the corridor the voices faded to an ominous silence.

Van's glance raced to the dead, ghastly face of Jud Marks outlined rigidly beneath the stained sheet. He leaped over to the narrow bed, tossed the bloody covering aside, carried the mutilated body to the operating table nearest the corridor door.

The G-man's body was limp. He propped it up facing the entrance through which the masked guards would come, managed to get the right arm and hand in a braced position so the lifeless fingers pointed accusingly straight at the door.

Outside, the key was scraping against the lock.

Van sacrificed his flashlight, turned it on and set it on the instrument tray so that its rays centered upon the grisly figure.

With a final swift movement, he turned out the powerful oil lamp in the room, sprang to the wall and flattened himself beside the steel door as it swung open.

A horrified oath broke from the lips of the first two guards as they rushed in. Their momentum carried them past the door, but the ghastly, spotlighted spectacle held them momentarily frozen in their tracks.

And in that split second, the Phantom plunged through the doorway out into the short, dimly lighted passage, his two guns pistol-whipping the five stunned guards outside!

He knocked three of them down before they could recover from the charging shock of his attack.

Springing past them, he reached the open elevator door, whirled into the car.

Both his guns blasted back into the corridor as flaming shots slugged at him. A masked guard screamed and flopped to the floor. A bullet nicked Van's knuckles as he jerked the door shut, grabbed the control lever.

The cage started down swiftly, the grating rattle of its descent drowned in the echoing barks of gun fire above.

Chapter Eleven
On Top

There was no guard at the bottom of the elevator shaft when Van stepped out of the car.

He made his way back to the big cavern where he had entered the unnumbered tunnel. The two hooded sentries were still posted there, but they let him pass when their torch lights showed the green circle with the two zigzag yellow stripes of an Empire officer on his black sleeve. Evidently no general alarm had been sent out for him, since he was supposed to be securely locked up in that subterranean concrete operating room.

The Phantom passed on into the main tunnel from which he and Jerry Lannigan had fled to make their escape from their original guards. He turned left, away from the direction of Vonderkag's gas cavern.

He was moving without a light, but the guards at the tunnel gates ahead of him, were satisfied with his officer's insignia and with the password, September Third.

When he had got by the last of the six doors he'd counted on his way in blind, he discarded the robe, mask and hood. A quarter mile further on he came to a fork in the shaft, and took the tunnel that had the heaviest bracing.

The passage climbed steeply, opened into a broader shaft up which ran a cog-wheel rail line for coal cars. There were no cars operating now. Van struggled up the long, sharp incline, came out upon a slag dump beneath stars and a bright moon.

He ran off the dump, darted along a mountain side, and dropped down to a dirt road. The fresh night air that filled his lungs gave him new energy. He followed the road, heard a railroad train laboring up a grade somewhere in the near distance.

Van had no definite idea where he was, except that he was in the heart of a coal mining district, probably in Pennsylvania. But fifteen minutes later, when he walked into a small town, his location assumed a grim significance.

The name of the town, Mountainview, was the post office address of the Alleghany State Penitentiary!

Van had Frank Havens on a long-distance phone connection to New York City within ten minutes. He was talking from a booth in the waiting room of the local railroad station. He didn't dare say much, and used the name of another Phantom alias, Jimmy Lance.

"I'll be at the Mountainview Hotel," he informed Havens. "Is Lannigan back yet?"

"He is," Havens stated. "And he'll fly me right out there."

"That saves me asking you to come," Van said appreciatively. "It's hotter here than you think. Bring along all the authority you can. If I'm not at the hotel there'll be a message for you. Anything else happened?"

"Yes," Havens told him tersely. "The Twin-City Power Dam at Minneapolis was destroyed by a blast-one single blast did it-to-night! And several more hooded men were reported seen at the disaster immediately after the explosion. The Twin-Cities are in a panic, partially without light, and the State Militia has been called out by the Minnesota governor!"

The Phantom kept back the flow of words that leaped to his tongue. One single explosion-the new explosive Kag had perfected!

Havens' voice came over the line again:

"I'm leaving for Mountainview at once!"

Van cut off the connection. Enough had been said over the phone. The clock in the hotel lobby showed ten P.M. when he registered for a room and locked himself in.

There was still time to visit the prison, if he could get inside the grim walls. Jud Marks' F.B.I. badge should help him there.

The Phantom spent five more minutes at the mirror and wash basin, removing the grime of the mines from his face, brushing off the blue suit he'd taken from Rotz. When he finished, he looked like a hard-traveled man who might have been a salesman.

It took him twenty minutes to get a local taxi and ride to the penitentiary on the outskirts of the town. The prison appeared bleak and grey, and fortlike in the night. It was built on a mountain side, one high stone wall almost abutting the rock-ribbed mountain itself.

About the tough prison was an atmosphere of menace and mystery that seemed to hover even over the wooded, thickly undergrown background of rugged ranges and deep, boulder-strewn valleys.

Van announced himself to the prison turnkey as a Federal agent named Jim Lance checking up on the escape of Snakey Willow, shot to death in New York City. He flashed the murdered Jud Marks' gold badge, asked to see the warden at once.

A rangy fellow named Rowan listened to the Phantom's preliminary questions irritably.

"Can't give you no information," the deputy grumbled. "You'll have to see Bluebold himself. He's in a huddle right now with Mr. Arnold who's Chairman of the Board of Parole. Dr. Jessup, the prison physician, and the wall and cell captains are with him. We got Killer Kline, that two million dollar mail robber and murderer, coming up here from Pittsburgh to be electrocuted next week. We do all the state's killings up here, since we built the big new chair."

Van studied Rowan's dull features keenly. The deputy wasn't impressed by the presence of Jim Lance, G-man, but was obviously in considerable awe of the Pittsburgh big shot who was to be locked up here for the last brief week before his official execution.

"Kline gets delivered here in the morning," the deputy went on, "so we ain't taking no chances on anything happening to him while he's with us, until he gets the jolt in the electric chair. Bluebold and the others are in the Board Room getting up their plans to handle this killer now. So you'll have to wait until they're done."

He took Van into the warden's office inside the prison behind the double gates of the turnkey's cage, and sat with him for a half hour until Bluebold and the men in the conference came out of the Board Room door at one end of the prison chief's office.

During that wait, Van's attempts to get the deputy to talk about the prison's management failed dismally. The rangy officer was obviously under orders not to give out any information at all concerning the activities behind these grim walls.

Rowan had run completely out of conversation when the Board Room door opened and the conference filed out.

The Phantom eyed the seven men in turn as they entered the warden's office. They were all big, powerful sharp-glanced, with the hard look of prison officials accustomed to handling convicts ruthlessly. The two cell captains and the two officers in command of the prison wall guards went out immediately. The deputy introduced Jim Lance, told what he'd come for.

In the austere environment of the penitentiary, Warden Jack Bluebold was even more rugged and capable looking than he had appeared when the Phantom had first seen him in Frank Havens' office. He sat aggressively in the chair behind his desk, eyeing Lance with shrewd, suspicious appraisal.

Ex-Congressman Harry Arnold, the Parole Board chairman, seemed no different than he had been in New York. His bearing was confident, his manner unruffled and assured. The responsibility of handling Killer Kline and electrocuting the tough murderer hadn't disturbed the politician's suavely alert and open-minded appearance.

Dr. Maurice Jessup, Van observed, seemed to be the only one of the three who was not fully satisfied with what had been decided upon in that Board Room meeting. He kept darting unexpected glances at Arnold and Bluebold, as though on the verge of declaring himself on some point which he never quite voiced.

The three officials were no more impressed by the presence of a G-man investigating Snakey Willow's escape than Deputy Rowan had been. They listened tolerantly to Van's questions, and Warden Bluebold became the spokesman.

"Snakey Willow was working in the foundry, welding a job, when some of the metal kicked back into his face. His welding glasses saved his eyes, but we had to patch up his ugly map or he wouldn't have had any face at all. Dr. Jessup's pretty proud of how he fixed Willow's face."

Dr. Jessup nodded. "I took my time on him," and shrugged. "Willow told me nobody'd know him, if he ever got out again."

Bluebold jerked open a drawer, thrust a printed "Wanted" police broadside at Van, The folder gave Willow's Bertillon and fingerprint measurements and his picture before the lifer had had his face lifted. The date of release printed on the police notice was four days old.

"Hell!" Bluebold exclaimed. "Deputy Rowan here, who was in charge of the prison while I was on a trip to New York, reported the escape as soon as it was discovered, and had that broadside sent out. I admit we've had some graft and corruption going on here under our noses, but we're getting that cleaned up. I fired eight inside guards today!"

"Yeah," Rowan nodded. "Those eight screws won't be sneaking in any more contraband."

"Besides bringing in whiskey on their hips," Dr. Jessup exclaimed caustically, "those guards were bringing in dope!"

Van handed back the police broadside to Bluebold.

"I'm not through cleaning up this prison," the warden declared determinedly. "But it takes time to ferret out these rats who've been wearing guards' uniforms around here. Mr. Arnold is going to appear before the state legislature with a bill that will make it a felony for a state penitentiary employee, guards and civilians both, to be caught carrying in or out anything that isn't permitted in the book of prison rules. The way it is now, all I can do is can these birds whenever we catch them trying to slip something over on us!"

The Phantom nodded, letting them talk.

"All they lose is their jobs," Harry Arnold emphasized. "We can't prosecute them. This is the toughest prison in the state, a sort of Alcatraz where the hardest criminals are sent. Those crooks usually have plenty of money and friends outside the walls, so you can understand, Mr. Lance, the profit there must be in bringing contraband in here to the prisoners."

Dr. Jessup, Warden Bluebold and Deputy Rowan jerked their heads in agreement, their eyes on Van.

"I'd be safe in saying," Harry Arnold went on, "as I'm going to say to the state legislature, that without a law putting a high felony penalty on such violations of our penitentiary rules, the crooked guards and civilian employees can, and do, make ten times their salary carrying in contraband and taking out uncensored letters to be mailed without our knowledge!"

Van asked bluntly, "How do you figure Snakey Willow got out?"

Warden Bluebold's eyes glinted. "Outside help did it!" he snapped. "This prison is escape-proof from within. There's a double count when the cons are locked in their cells at night, and again when they're let out to go to the shops in the morning. That count is checked twice each time before the cell doors are locked. At the shops and wherever the men work, there are between two and four guards who are responsible for the number of cons they handle. Willow's changed face might have helped, but you can't blame Dr. Jessup for that."

"If the guards are corrupted with money outside when they're off duty," Arnold put in, "all the warden and his deputies can do is wait until something arouses their suspicions, or until a convict disappears. We know the cons can't get out without help. It's the screws and the civilians who aid in the few escapes we've had. We're organizing a spy system among the guards themselves, which should help us detect crookedness before anything serious happens."

The four prison officials talked on, emphasizing what they'd already said, repeating themselves in different words. The Phantom recognized the hard logic in their statements, but could not break through the defense barrier they were building against him. The whole story was not coming out, whatever it was. They were ganging up on him, holding him off with reiterated generalities.

"How about the hospital?" he demanded. "Prison hospitals are apt to be a breeding place of corruption, due to the necessity for less iron-bound rules."

Dr. Maurice Jessup glanced at him with a gleam of contempt. "Perhaps that is true in other penitentiaries. It isn't true here!"

Warden Bluebold thrust out his jaw. "Our hospital is the hardest spot in this institution to get into. A convict is damned sick before he's admitted. We don't even allow visitors to go through that part of the prison without a special guard as a guide. Dr. Jessup is as much a disciplinarian as I am, besides being a very exceptional doctor and surgeon."

Van's eyelids flicked. They were putting this on heavy now-too thickly for him to swallow whole. There wasn't going to be a single loop-hole for him or any other investigator to use as a starting point.

He switched his attack, asked suddenly, "Ever had any trouble with any secret societies around here?"

The four men looked at him with set blankness in their eyes. Then Arnold chuckled good-naturedly.

"I see what you mean, Lance," he said tolerantly. "The papers are beginning to play up the old Ku Klux Klan idea in connection with the Arizona dam disaster. About twelve years ago, if I remember right, there was an organization of Ku Kluxers in these parts, but they sort of petered out after the national exposure of their political aspirations."

Warden Bluebold scowled. "If you're really investigating Snakey Willow's escape, Mr. Lance, you won't get anywhere chasing screwy newspaper scareheads. The payoff on that was cold cash on the line, outside, and not any nutty Ku Klux hocus-pocus. I'd suggest that you try to find the surgeon who fixed up Snakey's mug. That's the angle that Mr. Arnold, Dr. Jessup and myself are working on."

Van nodded, his veiled gaze hiding the sharp alertness behind his drooping lids. If that thermometer he'd found, with Alleghany Penitentiary stamped upon it, meant anything, Warden Bluebold's words were a direct challenge.

"I guess you're right, warden," he said, as though he'd begun to lose interest in the Willow case. "If you don't mind, I'll go through the prison tonight, so I won't have to wait over until tomorrow. I've got to make a routine report on this, anyhow."

"That'll be all right," Bluebold stated. "Deputy Rowan will show you around."

Van shook hands with them, then followed the deputy into the main corridor opening into the two big dormitory wings of the institution. Rowan seemed voluble enough now, so long as the Phantom stayed on generalities.

They walked along railed and lighted galleries past row upon row of gloomy cells in which the convicts slept restlessly. An occasional cry of some prisoner in his sleep was the only sound that broke the peculiar monotone of four thousand men breathing in weary nervous rhythm.

The great dining hall was a dark, deserted auditorium of long, narrow tables that gave the vague impression of deserted tombstones, where their footsteps shuffled ominously loud in the echoing silence.

In the shops, where shoes and cheap mining machinery were manufactured by convict labor, the rows of lathes, presses, cutting machines and drills were grotesque shapes poised in grim stillness, waiting for the maw of morning when they, would grind again into endless, heart-breakingly monotonous motion.

Van took particular notice of the enormous foundry as he and the deputy passed through its shrouded darkness. The high-ceilinged shop with its two big blast furnaces was peculiarly well equipped, and there were extra night guards stationed around its thick walls.

"That's the hospital over there," the deputy announced when they came out into the prison yard again.

He pointed at a four-story stone building set against the grey prison wall. It was dark, except for a red light over the entrance and a glow from one of the windows on the top floor.

"I'd take you in there," Deputy Rowan stated with finality, "except there's an iron-bound rule against visitors, official or not, going there at night. Black-Jack Bluebold would kick hell out of me if I let you in. Anyhow, the place is locked and I haven't got the key on me."

"Who keeps that key?" Van asked.

"Dr. Jessup, when he's inside the prison," Rowan answered and eyed Van distrustfully. "Other times it's locked up in the warden's safe. There's a fire exit that can be opened from inside the hospital, if that's what's worrying you."

The Phantom shrugged. There was no use his trying to break through the official reserve of these prison officials any longer. They were telling him just so much, and no more. But there was another way of getting past their loquatious, calculated barriers.

"Where's the death house cells?" he asked.

"See that light on the top floor of the hospital building?" Rowan said, his voice hardening. "That's it. There's two guys in there now, Sam Robbins and Joe Sholtz. We're frying Joe tonight. The electric chair is where that light shows. They're getting it ready."

The Phantom studied that grim window with the drawn shade a moment, his grey eyes slitted, his features masking the intensity of his sharp scrutiny. The shade of death would be drawn across that window in a few brief hours.

"I've seen enough," he said abruptly. "I'll fix up my report to the bureau from what information you've given me."

Relief showed on Rowan's face as they walked back to the main cell blocks and on through to the turnkey's double-doored cage.

Van thanked the deputy, shook hands with him, and was let out into the starry night. But the Phantom's eyes had become strangely restless.

Chapter Twelve
Fast Flight

When he got back to town Van stopped at an all-night restaurant. He had almost forgotten that he was ravenously hungry. But his mind was not on the food he ate.

He calculated the flying time from New York City to Mountainview, Pennsylvania, decided that Lannigan and Havens would land at the small local airport at about two o'clock in the morning. He needed sleep, but he could sleep in the plane, after he'd convinced Havens of the necessity for the queer, dangerous action he was planning.

Speed was essential; and next to that, Havens' influence as a public figure. He'd need Jerry Lannigan, too.

Van had left nothing at the hotel. He went directly to the airport from the restaurant, found the two small hangars locked and the field deserted.

He waited impatiently at the edge of the single short runway, keeping himself awake with cigarettes and frequent nervous pacings, while his mind went over and over the details of his plan.

At ten minutes past two in the morning, an hour and a half after the Phantom had reached the forsaken airport, he heard the first faint drone of an airplane motor. He stared skyward, caught sight of the red, green and white triangle of the ship's flying lights.

The moon was still out, making landing flares unnecessary. A half minute later the beat of the motor ceased and the ship drifted down toward the field, spiraling as Lannigan maneuvered for a short landing. The twin wing lights flashed on as the ship slid down and settled on the ground.

Van was at the door of the plane's cabin before Havens had it unlocked. He jerked it open, flashed his platinum and diamond insignia at the publisher, and pulled himself into the cabin.

"Get into the air again, Champ!" he ordered.

The roar of the motor as Lannigan taxied rapidly and turned into the wind, taking off again, gave Van a chance to greet Havens and slap the big red-headed Irishman on his beefy shoulder. When the ship was above the mountain ranges, leveling off, Van said determinedly to Havens:

"You've got to see the governor of Pennsylvania for me right away, Frank. Is he at the capitol in Harrisburg?"

Havens shook his head, reached forward and tapped Jerry on the arm. "Pittsburgh, Lannigan," he directed, and turned to Van. "Governor Young is in Pittsburgh tonight. I talked with him on long distance after Lannigan got through to me and said you were down in a Pennsylvania coal mine near Mountainview."

The publisher smiled wanly and added, "I wanted Young to have a detachment of National Guardsmen ready in that district, in case I didn't hear from you within the next twelve hours."

"That wouldn't have helped any," the Phantom declared flatly. "That region is honey-combed with connected mines, for miles around." He glanced at Lannigan, asked him. "How'd you get out, Champ?"

"I hung onto that elevator until it stopped," Jerry said over his shoulder as he banked and headed for Pittsburgh. "Then I got into the shaft bracing beams and climbed on up. I was still in the mine, but those hoods had disappeared, so I smacked a couple of guys that got in my way, and found a drift that led me out finally. Jeez, I had to walk about five miles to get to a phone. A miner drove me to the Mountainview airport and I chartered a plane. What happened to you after I scrammed?"

Van's eyes held a faraway look for a moment as he recalled the burly figure of Lannigan hanging to the bottom of that mine cage. Then he gave the two men a swift account of his own attempts to penetrate the hooded mystery.

As he talked, Frank Havens' age-lined face darkened into a frown of grim worry that matched the graveness of his steady gaze.

"Phantom," he said, "you've taken too many risks already." He looked down through the cabin windows at the dark, ragged tops of the mountains. "But we've got to keep on until the Imperator is stopped! Governor Young will use his soldiers —"

Van cut him off with a shake of his head.

"It can't be done that way, Havens," he insisted sternly. "Even if the entire district was surrounded, these members of the Invisible Empire could come and go as ordinary miners-most of them are workingmen who've been duped into joining this legion."

"Got to nail the bird who calls himself the Imperator," Jerry declared. "I was in those mine tunnels myself, and I know! You couldn't even blast 'em out with that stuff that blew up Rock Canyon Dam!"

"You see, Frank," Van went on, "the members are too afraid of their leader to talk, even to save themselves. And he knows that nothing can drive them out into the open so long as he remains an unseen emperor, and continues to pay them off. Remember, if any member is killed, that man's family is guaranteed financial independence for seven generations! It's a weird idea but it holds them, makes them willing martyrs."

"Can't he be cut off through his finances," Havens demanded. "Money can be traced!"

"Not the way he handles it, evidently," Van persisted. "Don't forget all the small bank robberies, the blackmail pay-offs, the things he can do with that explosive of his. And now he's going after the United States Treasury. You can't trace gold, you know. And he does not keep his money in public institutions, I imagine. That hospital room he's got underground, is proof enough he can, and probably does, have vaults buried in those tunnels."

"What's all this got to do with Governor Young, then?" Havens demanded. "You say you can't use state militia to any purpose."

The Phantom's grey eyes glowed. "The heart of this secret organization is in that prison at Mountainview, Frank, I've told you I made a pass at it tonight, and ran into a blank wall. But there's that thermometer with Alleghany Penitentiary stamped on it. There's the fact that three men from that institution were in your office at the time your man was to report to you on Dr. Junes' aluminum-calbite fusion experiments-and that man was murdered.

"There's the killing of Junes by these hooded devils, witnessed by Jerry and myself! There's the theft of that aluminum-calbite meteoric fragment from the Smithsonian Institute in Washington, and its delivery to Vonderkag down in the mines. The whole thing ties up with the fusion of these two metals —a fusion demonstrated as a possibility by that fragment itself!"

Lannigan called over his shoulder, "I'm with you, Skipper, whatever it is you're leading up to. Maybe you didn't get much chance to keep up with your reading, down in the mine, but the newspapers are reporting, now that two or three hooded guys were seen at that Mississippi River explosion in Minneapolis. Mort Lewis, remember the radio announcer, says he saw two of them hoods himself after the Rock Canyon blast."

The Phantom nodded to the publisher "Havens told me on the phone, and the Imperator boasted, in his speech down in the cavern, that the Arizona disaster had been a huge success for the organization, and that the new explosive-the stuff they used in Minneapolis-would be dropped from the air on the Treasury Building."

"All right," Havens said curtly. "The prison, you've discovered, is right on top of this mine district. What's your plan?"

Van looked searchingly at the publisher, and said "I want to get into that prison in the disguise of Killer Kline!"

Havens jerked in his seat. "That's an impossibility! Kline is the present Number One criminal in the United States. They're going to electrocute him almost as soon as they get him into the death house. He's to die some time during the week beginning September second-and that's tomorrow!"

"Yes, it's tomorrow," the Phantom agreed tensely. "And on September third, the day following, the Treasury at Washington will be blown up at dawn-if we don't stop the Imperator in the next" —he glanced at the clock on the ship's instrument panel —"fifty hours!"

For a long minute the grey-haired publisher pondered. Then he asked: "Suppose something goes wrong, Phantom? Suppose you're in there as Killer Kline, and they decide to hold the execution at once?"

Lannigan turned and eyed them. "They'd have a hell of a time, if I was there as a witness to that frying! And I'll be there!"

Havens' head moved slowly in negation. "You, nor anyone else, not even Governor Young himself, Lannigan could stop the warden if he should decide to strap Kline in that death seat at any hour after the week set for the execution starts."

"You mean, if somebody there-maybe the warden himself-got suspicious of Kline, or the Phantom?" Jerry demanded.

"That is exactly what I mean," Havens said. "The Phantom is convinced that the Imperator operates from within that penitentiary. If that is true, then the Imperator is one of those officials, or controls them. If he gave the word to electrocute Kline, nothing could stop that execution."

"Nothing can stop the Imperator's wrecking the financial heart of the country, until he's caught," Van insisted grimly. "I'm willing to take my chances in there." Defiance crept into his voice.

Havens eyed him sharply.

"In which instance," the Phantom added pointedly, "you couldn't ever be sure that I didn't manage to substitute myself for Kline. I could do it, you know."

A peculiar light, that had no malice in it, gleamed deep in the publisher's somber eyes. He smiled inwardly, but said sternly:

"That's a threat, Phantom. A challenge. I might even call it blackmail. In fact, it was I who asked Lannigan to fly us to see the governor in Pittsburgh."

"I'm glad you agree with me, Frank," Van grinned. "You can make things so much easier, when you quit fussing about my safety. Here's a few other things I'd like to have you work on while I catch some sleep. Get a line on the history of the executives and their assistants at Alleghany Penitentiary.

"And you, Jerry! Somewhere in the Mountainview district is a hangar, probably built under-ground like the new army field hangars. You won't be flying me back, but you can report to me as a visitor at the stir, and tell me how your hunt for that all-metal ship the Imperator has built is coming. Blow it up when you find it."

The Phantom's tired glance covered the two men a moment. Then he stretched back in the seat, adjusted the safety belt, and cocked Havens' hat over his eyes.

"Wake me up," he said, "when you get things fixed."

Chapter Thirteen
Killer Kline

It was six o'clock in the morning. Killer Kline was shaken awake and hurried from his cell in the Pittsburgh jail out a back exit into an armored car that sped him toward the airport.

In the car with him was another prisoner-the Phantom.

But that second prisoner had not been booked in any Pittsburgh jail. Van had been locked in the truck before it had left the sheriff's garage, as a precaution against spying eyes in the jail. Only the driver and the two guards-three special deputies assigned by Governor Young to make the Kline delivery knew that that second passenger rode in the steel box behind them. And even they did not know who he was.

Van studied the shrewd, ruthless features of the mail robber and machine-gun killer crouching on the iron bench in the armored box as the truck whirled through the streets. Kline's greenish grey eyes darted about the interior of the car ceaselessly, in search of a way of escape.

He was close enough to the Phantom in size, to make a switch a reasonable risk. Van's gaze noted brazenly the mannerisms of the criminal, the way he moved his hands, the leering twist of his lips:

"Going all the way?" he asked Kline bluntly.

"Not if I can help it," the murderer snarled. "They jolted Joe Sholtz up there in the stone house early this morning, didn't they? I ain't seen a morning paper yet."

"Yeah," the Phantom answered, getting the tone and inflection of Kline's sharp, harsh voice. "Four minutes it took to burn him dead. That's a long time to jerk against those death chair straps."

Beads of sweat began to stand out on Killer Kline's forehead.

"I do it in four seconds with a tommy gun," Kline growled. "It don't hurt so much, either. By God, I wish I had a tommy gun in my hands right now! They ain't going to fry me —"

He broke off, glowering at Van distrustfully.

"A smart, tough guy like you," Van encouraged, "shouldn't have to take the juice.

"Yeah." Kline's voice grated boastfully. "I ain't never stayed locked up long before. Parties make passes at me to get me out so I can help 'em pull jobs they ain't smart enough to do themselves." He shut up abruptly, eyeing Van with suspicion.

"I'll bet you got propositioned that way since you've been in the Pittsburgh can," the Phantom suggested.

Kline's gaze froze up. "I don't know what the hell you're talking about!" he declared belligerently.

Van didn't press him further. The Killer's manner implied that he'd already been approached with a chance to escape. It was what the Phantom had been expecting and hoping for.

A few minutes later the armored truck stopped at an outlying precinct station. The only door in the box opened and one of the three deputies called in:

"Come on out, Killer. This is as far as you go, this trip."

"What th' hell is this?" Kline demanded, and peered out the door. "This ain't the Alleghany stir?"

That was as far as he got. The deputies yanked him out of the car, manhandled him into the precinct station's alley entrance.

Nobody except Van and the three officers knew the transfer had been made. Kline would be booked under another name and hidden in a constantly guarded cellar cell until the Phantom or Governor Young sent word to have him finish his last ride.

The armored truck door slammed shut on Van and the car rolled off again. The Phantom forgot everything else for the next ten minutes as he concentrated on the make-up task confronting him. Before the truck reached the airport where a plane was waiting to fly Killer Kline to Mountainview, Killer Kline had to be reproduced.

From beneath his coat Van took out a paper sack containing the make-up kit he'd got on such short notice through the influence of Governor Young.

He set up a small pocket mirror, went to work swiftly. The Kline character had to be done entirely with the face, for Van would be stripped and re-dressed in prison clothes at the penitentiary. For the rest, he had to rely on his own ability to portray the Killer's characteristics in voice, mannerisms and action.

Fortunately, there were no Bertillon figures or fingerprints of Killer Kline on record at Mountainview. Those records would be taken there at the stir, and a copy of them mailed to the State and Federal identification bureaus-where they would be seized and promptly destroyed. Van had insisted upon that, to protect the Phantom's identity from being discovered. Later, if he survived the Alleghany Prison affair, the records there would be burned, too.

A moment before the truck swerved into the airport gate, a crumpled paper sack and a small pocket mirror fell from a gun slot in the steel car wall. The truck drove directly to a waiting ship, its door was opened, and Killer Kline was hurriedly transferred to the airplane.

There had been no hitch, no error. And there was none when the plane landed at the small Mountainview flying field and was met by a prison van.

Within thirty minutes Killer Kline was booked into Alleghany Penitentiary, without a hint of suspicion concerning his real identity, and the commitment papers were being signed by Warden Black-Jack Bluebold in person.

The same four men who had talked to Jimmy Lance in the warden's office the night before, now confronted the Phantom in the same room.

Ex-congressman Arnold and Dr. Maurice Jessup eyed Killer Kline in austere, watchful silence. Deputy Rowan, with three prison guards, kept the two doors into the office blocked. They were taking no chances with the notorious murderer.

"Still think you're the toughest guy in the United States?" Bluebold demanded harshly.

The Phantom put across his initial act with a snarl of defiance.

"I've got part of a week to live, starting tomorrow, you big punk! If you can think up anything during that time that's too tough for me, give me a crack at it, Peanut-brain! And that goes for the rest of you bottom rate chislers."

He swung upon them all. "Hell, there ain't a one of you smart enough to make yourself a buck outside. If it wasn't that the state paid you a salary, you'd all starve to death! Come on, let's take a squint at the death house you're so damned proud of."

"You'll take more than a squint at it, Killer," Bluebold snapped.

"Take him away and give him a bath, Rowan!"

But Rowan didn't take him alone. The three uniformed guards came along, crowding Van, yet watching him with nervous respect. He'd told off Black-Jack Bluebold! Killer Kline was the toughest con they'd ever handled.

Van shed his clothes, and took a secret satisfaction in making the muscles ripple under his skin as he moved about under the shower. These screws would think twice before they tried to maul him around. And his toughness and prowess as a hard guy would get talked about, which was what he wanted.

He wasn't sure the Imperator had sent an envoy to the real Kline in Pittsburgh jail. But he intended to give that mystery commander of the Invisible Empire a reason for wanting him as a member, if brazen courage and insolent fearlessness would do it.

Deputy Rowan threw him an outfit of prison clothes, drab, worn garments of faded muddy color that blended with the bleak, hopeless surroundings. Bluebold himself supervised the Bertillon and fingerprint records. Then he was herded over to the hospital.

Van's eyes sharpened as Dr. Jessup examined him, in the presence of the warden and Rowan and Arnold. The four men seemed to take a grisly delight in observing his physical qualifications.

"If you'd turned out to be a prizefighter or a professional wrestler, Kline," Dr. Jessup advised, "you'd have got some place in the world." He glanced at the others. "A wonderful specimen of a physique, gentlemen. It's really a shame to destroy it by electrocution."

"Count up the number of innocent and helpless guys Kline has killed," Harry Arnold said gravely. "Kline, you can't be executed but the one time. How many men do you figure you've murdered?"

"Who th' hell are you?" Van demanded. "Another punk screw?"

"Mr. Arnold," Bluebold said dryly, "is the Chairman of the Board of Parole and Pardons."

"If I added you to that list of guys I've rubbed out," Van rasped, "it would be a hell of a swell idea. Go on back to the Pardon Board and tell 'em that!"

"You're not going to ask Mr. Arnold for any help, I take it," Dr. Jessup remarked dryly.

"Nuts to him!" Van exploded. "I wouldn't take a pardon from none of you dopes. When I crash out of a stir, I do it my way!"

"Let's see you beat the death house, Kline," Black-Jack Bluebold challenged grimly. "I'll be waiting to shoot you!"

"Yeah!" Killer Kline snarled contemptuously. "You, with a gun. I can imagine! Hell, punk, I'd take it away from you and blow your damned face off with it!"

"Upstairs with him," Bluebold ordered.

The Phantom was ushered out of the prison physician's office into an elevator. There were no stairs, he noticed. At the fourth floor, which was the top, he was shoved out of the car into a steel-walled corridor at the end of which was a door painted a sickly green.

Bluebold, who had come up with him, pointed to the corridor's end. "That's the last door you'll ever enter, Kline. The chair is waiting for you on the other side. It's not a long walk."

Van did not answer. He'd put on his Killer Kline act enough, he imagined, and didn't want to overdo it. The guards shoved him into a cell, slammed shut the door which was entirely of steel bars.

There were seven other death cells on the corridor, four on each side, but none of them were occupied. Since Joe Sholtz had gone last night, Killer Kline appeared to be the only occupant of the death house.

But Deputy Rowan last night had mentioned a second murderer awaiting a future execution-Sam Robbins. And convicted men who entered this short corridor weren't supposed to be removed except through that fatal green door at the end, or by order of the Board of Pardons. If there'd been a pardon for Robbins, Governor Young would have mentioned it.

Robbins wasn't in the death house now.

Warden Bluebold and Rowan left him a few minutes later, after a whispered conference with the two guards on duty. The Phantom sat on the edge of the iron bed fastened to the wall, staring moodily through the bars at the empty cell opposite him.

He was on his own now completely. Not even Frank Havens could reach him on short notice, without the consent of Black-Jack Bluebold.

And suddenly Van remembered a mistake he'd made. He'd told Jerry Lannigan to visit him here, keep him informed about the hunt for the mystery plane. But Lannigan had been seen by the Imperator, or by several of the Imperator's men; in Dr. Waldo Junes' laboratory at Niagara Falls, and again in the mine, where Gulliver Vonderkag, the hunchback scientist, worked with the subterranean gas flame.

During those two periods, Lannigan had been stripped of the adhesive tape bandages over his eyes and mouth. And Jerry wore no disguise. If he showed up here, visiting Killer Kline, and one of the Imperator's men saw him-The Phantom shrugged off the thought of the consequences. At any rate, then the Imperator would guess the ruse that had been put over on the prison officials, and would show his hand in action.

Presently the elevator door jangled open and two men came into the corridor. Van could get only a passing look at them down the hallway, but they were in civilian clothes. He heard one of them mention his name: "Tough guy Killer Kline."

The two guards stepped over to his cell, unlocked the door, let in the two strangers, and locked the door again. Van heard them both go into the electrocution room beyond the green door, evidently so they wouldn't hear the conversation.

He stared at them sullenly, with the baleful contempt of Killer Kline himself. The two men were stocky, blunt-featured, shifty-eyed. They flashed state troopers' badges at him. They looked like brothers.

"Remember us, Kline?" one of them demanded.

The Phantom's eyes narrowed. Was this a trap? "So what?" he evaded. "I'm Garbo—I wanna be alone."

"Still the wise guy, eh?" the second one growled. "Well, you got this far along the route, sap. Want to let 'em fry you?"

"It's me that's gettin' fried, ain't it?" the Phantom snarled. He was stalling for time, trying to lead them into making some remark that would let him know what they were after, who they were. "I guess I got some rights left. If I wanna let 'em cook me, that's my business, ain't it?"

"That's what you said in the Pittsburgh can," the first of the two men grumbled. "You haven't got much time to make up your mind."

"I got a week," Van declared, eyeing them slantwise from the bed.

"That's what you think, chump. Listen!" The two men bent over him, as one of them prodded the air emphatically with a stubby finger: "Bluebold's got the authority to squirt the old juice into you any time after midnight tonight. Your last week starts then."

"Bluebold ain't in no hurry," Van exclaimed mockingly. "The publicity Killer Kline is bringin' him is plenty. He's eatin' it up!"

"Balance that publicity against the hundred grand you salted away out of that last mail robbery. It still adds up to cash on the line for your liberty. We ain't saying how soon Bluebold is figuring on watching you burn. He's sore. We offered you a chance at a proposition down in the Pittsburgh can. Want to talk business now?"

"You ain't very free with the details," Van growled.

The other stocky stranger elbowed his partner aside, and said:

"Look at the facts, Kline! For that dough, you get snaked out of here without any fireworks. You join up with our outfit and get an equity in your own money, and that's a damned sight more than you'd get trying to buy your way out through a regular stir delivery."

"Keep talking," the Phantom urged, and let himself show some growing interest.

Evidently Killer Kline had more of an inside track on his proposed escape than anyone had even dreamed. But Van still didn't know who these men represented.

"And another thing," the stocky man persisted. "You get taken care of after you get out of here. That comes with joining with us. The hideout is free, and you don't have to keep yourself locked up in no cheap room for a year, or keep jumping from town to town dodging cops, either."

Van spoke with a gleam of challenge in his sharp eyes.

"For a hundred grand you guys are going to make over the whole world so everybody'll love me or something? Me-the top killer of 'em all! Yeah, sell that plot to the movies, you lugs!"

"Don't get like that Kline," the second man grumbled. "You ain't heard it all yet. Our outfit's got a croaker that does the best job of face-lifting in the country. And he's working on a way to keep fingerprints from growing back again after he grafts new skin on the fingertips. All that medical stuff goes along with the hundred grand, soon as you join up."

"You won't recognize yourself, Kline," the first stocky stranger declared, "after that medico gets through with your map. You'd pay fifty grand alone for an operation like that, outside."

"Who's the croaker who does those operations?" Van demanded bluntly. "Why ain't I never heard of him before?"

"Yeah, a lot of smart guys would like to know that," one of the men told him. "Hell, Kline, we don't even know ourselves who he is. And what's more, we don't ask."

"And all my dough goes to that doctor?" the Phantom said.

"The dough goes to the organization, the mob," the other fellow told him. "You'll find out about it when the time comes."

"Gimme a little while to think about it," Van said after a pause during which they eyed him eagerly. "I'll probably come on in with you. But I gotta think about it." He saw their eyes cloud, and added quickly, "I can't pluck that hundred grand of mine out of the air in this damned stir. I'll have to figure how you can get it."

"Okay, Kline. You got until midnight tonight." The two men glanced confidently at each other. "You'll be seen before then, if not by us, by somebody who'll be in the know. And don't forget that midnight your death week begins. Black-Jack Bluebold ain't a nice guy to be waiting on, when it's your life he can burn up."

They rattled the door to attract the guards.

"Suppose I get quizzed about your visit," the Phantom said in a low voice. "What's the angle?"

"We're a couple of state cops, like our badges show," one of the men winked at him and grinned. "We're trying to find out what you did with that dough from that mail robbery."

The guard with the cell key let them out, and the elevator at the end of the corridor made a scraping noise as it took them down.

"Guard," Van called when the two men had gone. "Gimme a cigarette." And as the guard lit one and handed it to him through the bars: "Say, I thought I was having a guy named Sam Robbins for company. Where they got him now?"

"The prison physician, Dr. Jessup, moved him downstairs into one of the wards," the guard answered indifferently. "Sam complained that something he ate didn't agree with him. Then he got pretty blamed sick all of a sudden right after breakfast."

"Ate something that poisoned him, eh?" The Phantom's veiled gaze was sharp and hard behind the drooping lids.

Chapter Fourteen
Behind that Door

The Phantom had three more visitors that afternoon.

Congressman Harry Arnold was brought up by Deputy Rowan, who left immediately, and the interview was conducted with the bars of the cell door between them. Arnold was on his official dignity at first, but he became shrewder and more human as they talked.

"My purpose in coming here," the Congressman stated, "is to fulfill a formal duty. As Chairman of the Board of Pardons, I'm obliged to talk with every man condemned to death by the state, to make sure that he is given an opportunity to try for a pardon if his lawyer or friends or relatives have not done so."

Van stepped away from the bars and sat down on the end of the uncomfortable iron bed, studying the politician shrewdly. The man was rather handsome in a rawboned manner, and the inflection of his speech was flawless.

"I take my oratory sitting down," Van cut in on him. "After you get through about the pardon I couldn't get in a couple of million years, what're you going to talk about?"

Arnold raised his eyebrows appreciatively, and a faint smile twitched his lips.

"Aside from the fact that you're here in the death house, Kline," he said interestedly, "which means that you blundered —I'd say you were a pretty smart man. I suppose you won't be afraid to die, until the last minute or two. Or don't you give a damn any more?"

"What makes you think I don't?" the Phantom asked curiously.

Arnold shrugged mildly. "Your toughness, your hardness, Kline. The name you've acquired-Killer. Admirable qualities, sometimes. But-there's always the chair at the end."

"Nerts!" Van snapped at him. "I figure I'm in for a battle over that hundred grand I'm supposed to have tucked away-and what do I have to listen to? A sermon!"

"Dr. Jessup's point of view is rather apt," Arnold remarked, his glance still amused. "It ought to be a shame to destroy a specimen like you." He turned away abruptly toward the elevator. Over his shoulder he said, "I may see you again before Bluebold's nerves get the better of him. I'm afraid your reputation is working against you this time-speeding the last hour."

Van lay back on the bed, pondering. Arnold had been present in Frank Haven's office when the three officials from the Alleghany Penitentiary had appeared. That was about the only suspicion Van could attach to him.

Yet Arnold, being a politician, had to be a public speaker and organizer. It would take a shrewd organizer to build up and control such a fear disciplined mob of hooded devils as Van had run into.

Arnold didn't seem to possess the ruthlessness needed, hadn't evidenced such hardness at any rate. Nor had he displayed any knowledge of either medicine or chemistry-the two requirements the leader of the Invisible Empire must possess besides a genius for organization in secret.

Anyone, the Phantom reasoned, could hire a surgeon to transform the criminal faces of crooks who chose to become members. He was trying to consider the prison executives one at a time now, and kept Dr. Jessup out of the mentally probing picture for the moment. And anyone could hire a scientist, such as Kag, perhaps.

But the rub was, that no shrewd-minded commander of such a society as the Imperator controlled, would sensibly care to trust both of the main mechanical factors in his organization to hired men. He'd almost have to be an expert in at least one of the two major lines himself, over and above his executive capacity.

Van's thoughts were interrupted by the arrival of Warden Bluebold. Van stood up, leaned against the bars, eyeing the prison chief sharply.

"How do you like your temporary quarters now?" the big man asked. He handed Van a fresh pack of cigarettes. "The guards give you lights for your smokes and tend to your whims okay, Killer?" His attitude was not sour, but unexpectedly cheerful.

"I'm doing fine," the Phantom told him. "Decided when you're going to tuck me into the chair and turn on the juice?" He eyed the warden sharply. "Your pal Arnold is afraid I'm getting on your nerves."

"Arnold? Humph!" Black-Jack Bluebold's voice was a tolerant growl. "Mr. Arnold isn't tough enough, I'm thinking, to make a good prison warden. Kline, it takes guys with nerve-like you and me, Killer! I'm going to get a kick out of throwing the switch on you."

"Tomorrow morning?" Van asked pointedly.

"That'll be up to you, in a way," Bluebold told him flatly.

"Saving me for something?" The Phantom's voice was caustic.

"I want to find out where that money is you got on your last robbery, Kline. The insurance company put it at a hundred thousand dollars. Want to talk about it now-or later?"

The Phantom covered his own surprised reaction in a Killer Kline shrug of contempt. "I was waiting for something like that, you big punk! Personal shakedown, eh? Suppose somebody beat you to it?"

Bluebold's eyes narrowed dangerously.

"Kline, I've stood about all the insults from you I'm going to take! I can fry you at midnight tonight, and by God, if you don't control that dirty tongue of yours, I will turn the heat on you then!"

Van's voice cracked back at him:

"Why the hell don't you? What's stopping you? What the devil are you waiting for?"

The warden's face reddened. He started to shout something, but bit off the words with a snap of his heavy jaw.

"If you've got a proposition to make," the Phantom told him flatly, "let's have it, Bluebold. You ain't the only one making passes at me."

"Listen, you rat!" Bluebold growled, his eyes smoldering with hate, "I ought to come in there and beat that information out of you. But there's other ways of finding out." His manner changed suddenly, became icy and deliberate. "I'm not after that dough for myself. There were two dicks up here to see about that money a while ago. What did you tell 'em?"

The Phantom's eyes glittered. Was Bluebold in with those two phony state trooper detectives, afraid they were doublecrossing him?

"I told them," Van answered, "what I'm telling you, Bluebold! Before I cough up about any dough I may have parked somewhere, I want time to figure out where I come out on the deal."

"I see," Bluebold said stonily. "All right, sucker! Figure it out your way, but don't figure too damned long. Midnight tonight!" He strode away from the cell door, stomped heavy-footed into the elevator and went down.

Van began pacing the narrow cell floor.

He couldn't figure Bluebold out. The man was harder, tougher than Arnold. And he had a reputation as a ruthless disciplinarian-an essential requirement for a man handling any secret society like the organization that called itself the Invisible Empire.

The Phantom's mind kept reverting to that underground surgical room where he'd found the Alleghany Penitentiary thermometer. It was obvious that, if there was a connecting passage from the prison down to that operating room-and Van believed such a tunnel existed. Warden Bluebold would have the greatest opportunity to use it.

With a degree of medical and scientific knowledge that he might easily be hiding beneath his harsh outward bearing, Black-Jack Bluebold could be the Imperator.

Van was still thinking about the warden when one of the guards brought him his supper. And Van's third visitor didn't show up until almost ten o'clock that night.

It was Dr. Jessup.

"I'm going to ask you a favor," the M.D. said without preliminaries when he came up to Van's cell door. "You don't have to submit to my request."

From the way he said it, though, there was little doubt that Killer Kline would conform, or else!

"Going to try to make a specimen out of me?" Van demanded.

"I'm conducting some very detailed experiments and analysis of the effect of electricity on the human body and brain," Jessup explained gravely. "I want to examine you more thoroughly than I've done-before the electrocution. I'll make the other part of the tests and experiments, of course, when I perform the autopsy on you."

"Glad you're so cheerful about it," Van said sardonically.

The cold, distant eyes of Dr. Maurice Jessup surveyed him with sharp eagerness. "Very good, Kline. We'll go down to my laboratory."

He summoned the two guards, had the cell door opened, and the four of them got into the elevator.

"Of course," Jessup said as they rode down, "I do this with the consent of the prison authorities."

The car stopped at the basement, and the Phantom was ushered across a barren concrete floor into a three room laboratory that was a strange combination of operating equipment and electrical instruments. The two guards had come into the main laboratory and stationed themselves near the door.

"The X-ray pictures come first," Dr. Jessup said, and led Van into a smaller room on the right. The place was furnished only with a large X-ray machine, a plate cabinet, and the one chair used for seating the subject. "Be seated, please," Jessup directed.

The Phantom parked himself in the chair, watching the doctor move swiftly about the small, compact space. Jessup's cold eyes seemed to be watching everything at once, and there was no lost motion in his movements.

Van's back was toward a narrow door opening into the basement proper, and a screen blocked his view of the larger main laboratory.

"Damn!" Jessup exclaimed suddenly. "I'll have to get fresh X-ray plates. Just sit where you are, Kline."

The doctor seemed to have forgotten that he was preparing to examine a criminal convicted of murder and capable of murdering again. He hurried round the screen, out into the main lab. Van could hear his footsteps cross the floor to the third of the three rooms. A door opened and shut.

For almost a minute there was silence.

Then, without warning, a screaming voice shrilled somewhere out in the dimly lighted basement.

The Phantom leaped from the chair, reached the narrow door that opened directly into the basement. As his hand shook the knob, the voice sounded again, screaming words. "You tricked me! I'm making explosives for your brainless empire —I'll expose you —I'll-aaahhh ! —"

The frenzied words broke off in a piercing wail of terror that chopped off into abrupt, ominous silence, punctuated by the thud of a falling body.

Van's hand jerked away from the locked door. He swung round the screen, saw one of the guards still standing by the main door, poised, a gun in his hand. The other prison guard was running out into the basement. Dr. Jessup was nowhere in sight.

The Phantom ran into the large laboratory as the second guard snapped out of his paralyzed posture. The two of them rushed out toward the uniformed screw bending over a huddled figure on the basement floor.

"Who is it?" the running guard shouted.

"Don't know," the other called. "Never saw him in my life."

But Van had seen that odd, grotesque form before.

It was Gulliver Vonderkag!

The Phantom stared down with narrowed, unbelieving eyes at that hunchback German scientist. The crippled man was already dead, but as Van and the two excited guards bent over him, no wounds or marks of violence were visible.

Remembering the gas fumes that had knocked him out in Dr. Junes' laboratory, the Phantom stooped suddenly between the guards before they could stop him, smelled Kag's lips, depressing the no longer breathing lungs. But there was no odor of gas, no sign of the purplish discoloration of asphyxiation.

The two guards yanked him back away from the body, and the two of them lifted the dead hunchback, carried him away into Jessup's laboratory.

As they laid the body on one of the operating tables, the prison physician emerged from the smaller room on the left, opposite the X-ray office. Dr. Jessup was carrying a packet of X-ray plates. He stopped, stared at the tableau, hurried over to join them.

Van eyed the doctor covertly, noted that the man's seeming surprise was replaced almost at once by a sharp, professional interest.

"Who is this man?" he demanded. "What happened?"

"We don't know," one of the guards exclaimed. "We heard a screech and some screw hollerin' about explosives —"

"I heard that part of it myself," Jessup declared, shutting off the guard's answer. "Thought it was a patient in a fit, up on the floor above." He glanced sharply at Van. "Where were you?"

"Right where you parked me, Doc!" the Phantom snapped. "What killed him?"

Jessup set down the plate case, started examining the body, while the others watched him. The doctor's fingers moved expertly over the dead cripple, removing the clothing, prodding, probing.

When he'd finished, he glanced up, frowning.

"Not a mark on him," he said. "Not a scratch!"

"A guy don't scream like that just from heart failure," Van remarked and stared keenly at the dead face.

Those wide eyes that had rolled so terribly in Kag's head were fixed now, concentrated straight ahead in glazed contemplation of eternity. Staring down at their vacuous expression, the Phantom's keen gaze caught a tiny fleck of blood that looked like a thread thin blood-vessel on the white eyeball. He bent over the still, agonized face, pushed the wrinkled flesh away from the eye socket.

"Mind, doc?" he asked, but didn't wait for permission.

On the outer corner of the left eye was a minute blood clot covering a needle hole that had penetrated the brain.

Van pointed it out to Dr. Jessup, noticing the worried, lines that appeared on the surgeon's features.

"Maybe the guards can find the needle that made that puncture," the Phantom suggested boldly. "Anyhow, Doctor, it took a medical man to know how to kill a guy that way."

Dr. Jessup looked at Van sharply, startled, but was too slow to stop him as the Phantom stepped back and crossed to the small room from which the doctor had emerged a minute after the murder.

Van reached the open door, stared swiftly through. A man moving fast could have got out of that room through a door, met and killed Kag, and got back into the room again before even the paralyzed guard could have seen him.

He scowled, stared again through that open doorway. A single glance covered the whole of the small room. There was not a door or a window in it, and the walls, like the walls of the other rooms, were of solid concrete.

Dr. Jessup couldn't have got out of there unless there was a trick door. Van had no chance to search for one. He was still Killer Kline.

Chapter Fifteen
The Voice

As the Phantom swung back into the main laboratory, heavy, quick footsteps sounded out on the basement floor, and a moment later Warden Black-Jack Bluebold stood staring at them all through the doorway.

"What the hell's going on down here?" he demanded angrily.

Then his eyes saw the naked hunchback on the operating table, the clothes strewn on the floor. His gaze hardened and his face became rocky as he advanced into the room. But by neither expression nor gesture could Van detect recognition in the beady-eyed prison chief's manner as he stared down at Vonderkag's white face.

Dr. Jessup told him grudgingly what had happened, and why Killer Kline was present. Still, the stolid features of the warden betrayed no emotion other than anger and resentment. Bluebold was either a consummate actor, or else his thick-skinned reactions were limited to ruthless malice.

"Where's Rowan, that damned deputy of mine, the lazy devil!" Bluebold growled. "I want this body got the hell out of here in a hurry! What am I running here, a prison or a madhouse?"

"How about finding out who killed that hunchback?" Van demanded.

"Yeah?" Bluebold's beady gaze glittered dangerously. "Since when did Killer Kline start worrying about catching murderers? You shut up, or I'll hang this bump-off onto you!" He went to one wall, grabbed the phone receiver off its hook, barked into the instrument:

"Get me my office, Muldoon-Hello, Rowan? —Send a guard detail down to the hospital basement. Man killed here —I don't know-Oh, he is, eh? Be right up."

He turned back to Jessup. "Arnold just came into my office. Wants us to bring Killer Kline up there right away."

"We'd better go along then," Dr. Jessup said. "I'll finish with Kline afterwards."

"If we don't fry your specimen first," Bluebold said sourly.

Van went with them through a heavy door in the hospital basement wall, down a flight of steps into an underground concrete connecting passage, electric lighted, that brought them out into the corridor behind the warden's office.

Rowan and Harry Arnold were alone in Bluebold's private room when the three of them entered.

"Lock Kline in the Board Room with a couple of guards," Arnold said curtly. "I've got a surprise for you." He smiled blandly at the prisoner. "We'll let you in on our surprise in about ten minutes, Killer."

Jessup was repeating the circumstances of the killing, back in the hospital, to the Pardons Board chairman when Rowan took Van into the Board Room through the door that opened from the warden's office. Rowan put two guards in with the Phantom, went back and joined the other three men.

Van borrowed a smoke off one of his guards, began wandering about the long, high-ceilinged room. Bookcases containing the bound laws and penal records of the state lined one wall. Opposite were full length pictures in oil of the state governors over a period of more than a hundred years.

A long oak table with stiff chairs pressed against it occupied the center of the room. Two tall heavily barred windows at one end of the room gave the only outside light-showed now dark night sky above a row of gloomy pines.

The impression the room gave was frigid, ominously bleak for those condemned men who faced the Pardons Board here to argue for their lives. But for the Phantom, as he moved around the gloomy room, the place seemed to exude a sinister, premonitory warning.

The murderer of Kag, under the hospital, had disappeared as though the walls had swallowed him. Yet that killer had left a clue, the deft mark of a medical man. And Kag's last shrieking words had irrevocably tied that unseen murder to the Imperator in a binding union of identity that could never be broken.

But of the Imperator, the killer of Kag, there was still not the slightest trace. Van had been so positive, for a moment, that Dr. Maurice Jessup was the man, that the weird, grim mystery of the Invisible Empire had seemed to solve itself in a single flash of comprehension. And then there had been no visible second door out of that one basement room. The obvious and narrow deduction that Jessup had killed Kag had become a problematical, unproved chance again!

What, now, was going on in the warden's office, Van had no idea. One of the guards was stationed near the door, barring him off from any attempt to listen at the panel.

Had he been alone, the Phantom would have searched even this austere room for a possible secret opening into that hidden passageway which Van was positive existed, connecting the prison with the subterranean operating room and the labyrinthian mine shafts below. He had to content himself, under the hard, suspicious eyes of the two guards, with spotting possible likely places where such an exit might be concealed in the long room.

The door to the warden's office swung open abruptly, and Deputy Rowan appeared, his eyes burning grimly at Killer Kline.

"Come on in," he rasped, and snapped at the two guards:

"You screws beat it."

Van watched him let the guards out into a corridor exit. Rowan locked the door again, nodded at him. "Okay. Let's go!"

The Phantom entered the warden's room, and the Board Room door locked behind him. He faced Black-Jack Bluebold who glowered at him from across the heavy desk. Jessup and Arnold were standing to one side, and Rowan joined them.

"Well, Killer Kline," Bluebold grated, "this is the end for you!"

"Going to fry me tonight?" the Phantom asked harshly.

The four men nodded.

Van's eyes slid over the room-furniture, walls, ceiling, doors, barred windows. There wasn't a chance to escape! And there was neither pity nor patience in the four pair of grim, ruthless eyes glaring at him. In the tight, watchful silence of the office, the only human element of contact seemed to come from the faint, metallic hum of the radio in the corner where it had been turned down but not quite off.

"We've decided," Bluebold stated in a deadly voice, "that the sentence imposed upon you by the trial judge in Pittsburgh will be carried out one minute after midnight tonight! Thirty-five minutes from now." He glanced at his watch. "Anything you've got to say, Kline?"

Van stepped closer to the desk. "Lemme write a note," he said. "You can read it."

"Stalling?" Bluebold asked sharply.

"It's about that hundred grand I'm leaving behind," Van said.

"We're not interested in that —" Bluebold started, but the politician broke in on him with:

"Write the note, Kline! It's his privilege, warden. That hundred thousand dollars belongs to somebody."

The Phantom glanced about him as he picked up a sheet of stiff writing paper. Dr. Jessup was picking up the phone, starting to give orders about his medical kit being taken up to the execution chamber. Rowan was on another phone, giving directions to the guards who would be on duty during the licensed killing.

Van's gaze flicked and his lips twitched.

"Getting nervous, eh?" Bluebold sneered.

"Not much." The Phantom put fear into his voice, and suddenly slid the sharp edge of the paper across his thumb. "Hell! I guess I must be getting jittery —"

Blood spurted from the deep cut, smeared the edge of the warden's desk, made crimson blotches on his papers. Bluebold swore, jerked open a drawer, slapped a first-aid kit on the desk top, pulled out a roll of bandage.

Van held out his hand, thumb up, watching Bluebold keenly. As the warden began wrapping the bandage around the cut, the Phantom jerked his hand awkwardly, wincing.

Bluebold cursed and the bandage slipped off onto the desk.

"Here!" Arnold snapped. "Let me, warden. You're as nervous as he is." He caught the bandage in his fingers, wrapped it securely, twisting it around Van's wrist. "All right, Kline. You won't need to wear it after your heart stops beating."

"Thanks," the Phantom said. His voice had a sudden steely ring. "Before I put on this party, suppose you let me in on the surprise you've got."

"Sure, sure, Kline." Bluebold glared at him. "Part of that little surprise is something maybe you can help explain, Killer. You've got some queer friends."

"Bring him in," Arnold advised. "Let's get it over with."

Bluebold punched a button on his desk. There was a brief pause. Then a key grated in the lock of the corridor door. It swung open with a bang.

Four burly prison guards crowded into the office, holding a fifth man-Jerry Lannigan!

The Phantom's narrowed eyes smoldered and he fought for control of his tensed, twitching muscles as he recognized the big, powerful, red-headed Irishman.

Lannigan's face was raw from a beating, but his blue eyes blazed defiance. He growled a curse at the screws holding him, and his gaze settled on Killer Kline.

"Know this guy?" Bluebold roared at Van.

For a fraction of a second, the Phantom hesitated, trying to signal Jerry to silence. But Lannigan's jaw was already clamped shut.

"Hello, Champ!" Van called to the burly fighter. "Thanks, pal, for the try!" He turned swiftly to Bluebold and the others. "Sure I know this bird. Champ O'Hara, from Frisco. He's an airplane pilot, and he was going to make a pass at chiseling me out of this stir. What tripped you, O'Hara?"

"Hiya, Killer," Jerry growled disgustedly. If he'd forgotten that one or more of these men might have seen him twice before, he'd now caught Van's cue, was putting on a swell act. "I cracked up my ship, and was trying to swipe a new one."

A wry grin split his bloody face as he went on:

"Did I pick out a good one, or didn't I? Jeez, it turned out to be a sort of kind of earthquake an' volcano! The damned thing blew up on me, Killer! Blew all to hell —"

Van's slatey eyes flicked. Lannigan had found that mystery ship, and demolished it!

"Tough going, Champ," he offered. "What was the trouble?"

"She was loaded with bombs, or something worse," Lannigan declared. "I found some airplane tracks in a deserted field, and there was this brand new crate hid in an underground hangar. It looked like what I wanted, so I went after it. Some hoods tried to shoo me off with gun slugs, but I had a rod and tossed some back at 'em. The ship didn't get hit, but I guess some of the bombs they were loading did. When I come to, Killer, the birdies was singing and I was asking for Killer Kline."

"Looks like you found me," Van said, and noticed that a deathly silence had fallen over the tensed office.

Black-Jack Bluebold was watching them both, catlike. Every eye in the room was on them.

Van saw the guns appearing in the hands of the four guards. Rowan and Jessup were edging toward him. Bluebold was getting to his feet behind the desk, fingering a long, sharp paper knife with a steely, ragged-edged blade.

Ex-Congressman Arnold's eyes were bleak as he moved away from the Phantom and Lannigan, toward the wall, his voice calling across the stilled room:

"Warden, this is your affair! I'd suggest you lock O'Hara up until you're officially finished with Kline." He jerked his head significantly at Lannigan. "Dr. Jessup, it looks like you've got a nice big new human specimen."

"Yeah!" Bluebold grated. "I'm running this pen! I'm frying Kline, and his tough gorilla pal can be a witness. Then I'll tend to him! Let's take 'em up, men!"

The broken silence of the office became a quick, restless stir. Across the room Van saw Jerry's blue eyes begin to burn and his neck muscles bulge. Bluebold was advancing, the knife held low, poised.

"It won't be your thumb that's cut this time, Killer!" the warden rasped. "I'm going to make your innards trail from here to the electric chair!"

The Phantom's eyes flicked at Lannigan again, and his face slid sideways, his jaw hunched close to his shoulder, his lips parted in a voiceless snarl.

And suddenly, from the corner of the office where the radio still hummed in dull, mechanical monotony, a metallic, chilling flow of words poured into the room:

"Attention, members of the Invisible Empire! Alarm! Calling the Imperator! Gas has broken into the officers' cavern! Warning! Calling the Imperator! Danger of explosion!"

The lights in the warden's office blinked off abruptly. The voice stopped. Instantly, the room became a pandemonium of shouts, curses, bodies hurtling into each other, fists thudding, screams.

A steel door slammed across the room, crackling like a pistol shot above the bedlam.

The Phantom hurled his lean body through the crowd, his hands pawing aside the blindly fighting, panicked men in his path as he leaped toward the sound of that door. His voice roared:

"Champ! Champ!"

Then his fingers clawed open the exit that had crashed shut, and he darted through, found himself in the darkness of the long, high-ceilinged Board Room.

Across in the blackness his narrowed eyes caught the vague movement of one of the full-length oil pictures as it swung shut against the wall.

As, he sprang toward it, he heard Jerry Lannigan's harsh breathing behind him.

Chapter Sixteen
Hell's Goal

Van reached the picture he'd seen move in the darkness. He ripped at its frame, swung it away from the wall. He pulled himself up into the black opening behind the canvas, reached out and touched Lannigan's groping arms.

"In here, quick!" he whispered.

Back of the big Irishman, across the length of the Board Room, the guards and prison officers inside the warden's private quarters were ham-mering at the steel door that Lannigan had slammed after him. The Phantom pulled Jerry up into the narrow hole behind the oil painting, swung the frame shut against the wall again.

"Here's a ladder," he muttered as his dangling legs knocked against iron rungs. "Got a light?"

"That's all I got!" Jerry growled. Van was already climbing down into the black well hidden in the Board Room wall. Above him, Lannigan's electric torch sent down a wavering, eerie glow as Champ followed him.

The hole seemed bottomless, but the Phantom didn't take time to listen for the sounds of that fleeing figure who had preceded them. Their own rapid descent made hollow, echoing thunder in the narrow well as their feet struck each iron rung.

When Van's feet hit solid dirt, finally, all noise from above had ceased.

Lannigan dropped down beside him, shifting the dim, fatigued gleam of the flash.

"Gawd!" he exclaimed. "Those guys up there don't know about this hole!"

"Lucky for us," Van said tersely. "A dozen shots pouring down would have finished us. Come on, Champ. Through here!"

A low opening in one side of the well let them crawl on hands and knees through a down-grade, twisting tunnel. Van reached back, took the electric torch from Jerry, crawled on ahead rapidly. Behind him, the beefy Irishman was having a tougher time getting his bulk around the sharp curves.

Then the tunnel widened, dropped off abruptly into a chasm.

Van's flashlight beam petered out into darkness before the glow touched bottom. He flung the beam across the empty space, centered it on a plank on the other side.

"Smart lad," he muttered to Jerry "He pulled his bridge across after him."

"Well, we can't sit here and catch him," the Champ growled.

Van measured the gap with a sharp eye. It couldn't be leaped without at least a short run. And nobody could run out of that hip-high tunnel through which they'd just squirmed their way.

"Might swing you over," Lannigan ventured.

The Phantom shook his head grimly and suddenly stretched out full length, his feet against one side of the passage, his hands against the other. By stretching out, he could make the long reach and brace himself a little.

"You may have to stay here, Champ," he warned. "If I miss!"

Then, stretched horizontally, Van began inching his body out over the chasm. Lumps of loose dirt slipped through his fingers, dribbled silently into the fissure, making no sound against a bottom too deep to send up even an echo.

Lannigan, watching him, began to sweat.

For a full half minute the Phantom was a straining human bridge from wall to wall above that bottomless pit. Then he dropped to the tunnel bottom on the other side. He took a deep breath, shoved the plank across for the Irishman.

Lannigan crawled over to him, pulled the plank back.

They went on, standing upright now in a higher passageway. And as they stumbled on, the Phantom began to recognize some of the landmarks he'd spotted during his escape from the mines.

He led Jerry on, down grade, twisting, turning.

"Where'd that devil go?" Jerry panted as Van hesitated a moment at a fork.

"He's headed for the water gate," the Phantom answered. "He thinks gas has broken out somewhere down below." Van spotted the turn he wanted, ran on again.

The gate to the elevator shaft Van was looking for almost broke as they crashed into it, but the car was at their level. They leaped in, started down.

"We'll split off from each other at the bottom," Van directed. "You take the left tunnel, follow it straight through to the third door, and turn right. You'll come out into the cavern where that water door is fastened into the cement retaining wall. I'll probably be there ahead of you."

"Suppose you're not," the Champ demanded.

"Then you'll run into this Imperator yourself, Jerry. I guess you'll know what to do with him. Pull a Frank Buck on him, Champ."

"I'll bring him back," Lannigan promised, "conscious, but in pieces, if you say so, Skipper. How do I know him when I see him."

The Phantom chuckled.

"You'll know him, all right. He'll be wearing a gas mask, and that damned robed outfit. But he won't have a white mask. If there's more than one, pick on the bird with the gas mask, Champ, and you can't go wrong."

"Okay," Lannigan agreed. "But where're you going?"

"I'm going to try to beat you there."

The elevator car hit bottom, stopped. Van grabbed Lannigan's hand in a firm grip. "Good luck, Irish. But if you hear water, run like hell! Get out any way you can!"

The pressure left Jerry's hamlike palm, and the electric torch was thrust into the Champ's fingers. Then the Phantom was gone, moving swiftly through a wide, dark passageway straight ahead of the elevator shaft.

He felt his way along, touching one side of the tunnel with his hands, feeling the ground ahead for his unseen footing. He wasn't positive, was relying upon his knowledge of mine tunneling, to locate the shortcut that reason told him should be here.

If he didn't find it, he'd have to run back and try to catch up with Jerry before the Irishman got to the cavern and the steel water barrier. But he'd sent the Champ on that route for another reason-to have a way cleared for a running escape. Lannigan, he knew, wouldn't leave anyone behind who'd have an ounce of fight left.

Then, two hundred yards from the elevator shaft, the Phantom found what he was hunting. It was a drop-off in a narrow shaft, leading at right angles from the main passage.

He could tell by the type of bracing his hands encountered that he'd guessed accurately. He was moving through an auxiliary shaft that served as an emergency exit into the mine further on.

Van slid down the sharp incline of the drop, bumped his way along uneven down-grade steps cut into the dirt, and emerged into a wider passage that opened suddenly into the cavern he wanted.

Even in the blackness, he could discern the feeling of movement in the air about him. Labored, harsh breathing guided him across a blank space where his hands touched only heavy, moist air.

As he advanced, crouching, a thin shaft of bright light slid along the further wall, caught and hung for a moment on a concrete foundation, then slid on again to circle the round steel water door.

The Phantom's pulse calmed now. He moved forward cautiously, silently. The light ahead blinked out. There was a prolonged silence. Then a dry creaking sound.

Van reached the concrete wall, flattened against it, edging closer to the steel door. He could hear the quick, hard gasps of breath again, each followed by another straining, louder creak of metal against unoiled metal.

And suddenly the torch flashed on without warning, skidded over the door, caught the Phantom full in the face.

Blinded by the unexpected ray, Van dove straight at the light. His shoulder hit a shifting human body, and his hands closed in on the familiar feel of a long robe.

Then the electric torch crashed down on his skull!

The Phantom twisted, half stunned and ducked a second blow as the light shattered into intense blackness. He slugged upward, hammering into a flat, hard stomach.

Then fingers gripped his throat, tightened.

With a wrenching lurch, Van threw himself sideward, tried to claw off those throttling fingers. He could feel his own senses reeling. The fingers, clawlike, closed down.

The Phantom relaxed abruptly, let his whole body go limp.

But the next moment, as the robed, writhing weight floundered down on top of him, his knees doubled under him, his heels kicked out, hit solid bone.

The crack of that blind kick was like the snap of a whip. He hung onto the cloth in his fingers, was jerked forward onto his chest, sprawled across the suddenly inert form beneath him. His fists smashed into an unprotected jaw with crunching force. There was no answering struggle.

But beneath him, now, was a trickle of water, and filling the cavern was a suppressed but growing rumble.

Van lunged to his feet, grabbing the limp figure. He half dragged, half carried it back toward the tunnel exit, shouting once more for Lannigan.

An answering bellow drowned out for a moment the increasing roar of the still dammed water.

"Skipper! Skipper!"

Then Jerry Lannigan's feeble torch gleamed in the darkness ahead, the weak rays caught Van's struggling figure.

A moment more, and the Champ was at Van's side.

"Carry this fellow!" the Phantom gasped. "Run! The bulkhead is breaking open!"

He grabbed the torch from Jerry, ran beside him. They reached the first incline at the cavern's exit as the water lapped at their heels. As they got into the tunnel, the dull growl back of them broke into a violent, angry roar.

"There it goes!" Van shouted. "The bulkhead gave way!"

They had a fair start, for the narrowness of the tunnel acted as a brake against the crowding water of the subterranean flood. And the up-grade helped beat the churning wall of dank water that, lunged at their heels.

But the flood was knee deep when they reached the elevator shaft, and waist deep before the creaking cage dragged them up out of the roaring, clutching current.

As the car climbed, Van jabbed the light downward through a crack in the flooring. The beam reflected only churning, rising water.

"That," he said, standing up again and putting the beam on the robed and hooded figure Lannigan was holding, "is the end of the Invisible Empire, Champ. They're finally, flooded out."

He lifted the head of the man slung limply over Lannigan's powerful shoulders, and jerked the gas mask off that pallid face.

"And this —" He shoved the light close to the no longer robust but now sagging features.

Jerry Lannigan said, "Yeah, I guessed who he was already. Warden Bluebold! It couldn't have been Jessup, the prison croaker, because I slugged him, chasin' you into the Board Room." The Champ grinned proudly at his own smartness, and turned his head to look.

A chuckle broke from the Phantom's bruised lips as Lannigan, his blue eyes widening, stared into the face of ex-Congressman Harry Arnold!

Chapter Seventeen
The Phantom Fades

Minutes later they were still in the mine, but the flood was swirling unseen, deep in the shafts below them. Lannigan was shifting Arnold's inert body on his shoulder when Van announced:

> "Here's the passageway I've been looking for, Champ. I came up here on another elevator, but there had to be some back way in, because there was a locked door I couldn't get out of."

He stood facing a steel door set in concrete-the rear entrance to the underground operating room-after they'd gone a few rods up a sharp incline. An up-elevator opened several yards further on.

The Phantom examined the lock on the door, took keys from Harry Arnold's pocket. One of the keys fitted, opened the door.

Van stepped swiftly across the threshold, got a light lit and stared about the Imperator's operating room. Only one thing in it had been changed since he'd escaped from there last:

The place of the dead, nude body of the F.B.I. operative, Marks, on the operating table was empty now, but a live man occupied the narrow hospital bed behind the screen.

As he crossed to that bed, the Phantom said over his shoulder, "Champ, get some tape and do a job on Arnold, but leave his mouth free." Then Van looked down at the new occupant of the room.

The man on the bed was stocky, dark-skinned, with dark, glittering eyes that darted over the Phantom's face in startled, hopeful recognition. His hands and feet were shackled to the bed, and his mouth was taped, but he had not been touched yet with a knife.

The Phantom worked the tape off the fellow's lips, stood back, waiting for the man to get his tongue moving again. A mumbled volley of oaths spewed from the prisoner's throat, and his words became rapidly intelligible.

"You're Killer Kline, ain't you!" he declared as soon as the profanity wore out. "The toughest crook of us all, eh? What'd you do, crack this stir?"

Van turned without speaking, set the screen aside so the fellow could see Lannigan and the Imperator in the robe and black hood. The man's eyes smoldered, then burst into darting flames of fresh hate:

"Him! The dirty, sneakin' —"

"Who're you?" Van barked.

"Me-you ain't forgot me, from the Pittsburgh jail! I'm Joe Sholtz. God! That guy you got there, he was going to skin me alive, he told me, so's he could use my hide on you, Killer! He was goin' to do a face-liftin' job on you, use you for somethin' he was planning. That's why I wasn't cooked in th' hot seat last night." Terror suddenly pitched Sholtz' voice. "You ain't gonna let him skin me now, are you, Killer?"

Van thought fast, sizing up the hard-looking con on the bed.

"I won't, if you'll talk," he snapped. "Maybe I can get you free of the hot seat, get 'em to commute your sentence to life."

"I'll tell every damned thing I know!" Sholtz declared. "I've been in this stir awhile. I seen some queer things."

"How'd you know it was Arnold who brought you here?" Van asked.

Sholtz' glittering eyes darted to the ex-Congressman's taped body. "The dirty rat! He was dressed up like the prison surgeon when he took me down here, handcuffed. He didn't think I'd ever get out. He took off the gauze he was wearin' over his face, after he'd chained me to this damned bed, so he could talk better."

Van turned to Lannigan. "Champ, that elevator out there'll take you up —"

"It'll take you up into the prison hospital basement," Sholtz cut in. "Lets you out through a fake dumbwaiter. But there's a halfway landing up the elevator shaft that opens into a tunnel leading to a rock quarry outside the prison walls. I was brought down from the hospital, but you can skip th' stir that other way."

"Get that?" The Phantom nodded to Jerry, who'd finished with Arnold's bindings. "Use that quarry exit, Champ. You'll find Havens with the National Guards the governor sent up to Mountainview. Tell them to take over the prison, and bring Havens, Bluebold, Jessup and the militia commandant back here with you. Lock up Deputy Rowan and his screws until we find out how much they're in on this."

Lannigan grinned, went out, and when Van had locked the door he swung back to Sholtz. "Who told you about that quarry tunnel?" he demanded.

"The hood who was with Snakey Willow on that New York killing," Sholtz said grimly. "He came in here that way, an' Arnold jumped him for using that entrance. I seen and heard the whole thing."

The Phantom's eyes flashed. "What happened?"

"The guy come in here and met Arnold," Sholtz growled. "And give him a briefcase snatched from the fellow shot in New York-Grand Central Station, he said, was the spot. Arnold raised hell because the thing had been bungled, and stabbed the hood to death right here in front of me. Gawd, it was bloody!"

Harry Arnold had opened his eyes and was staring at Killer Kline with growing comprehension and fear. Van turned on him:

"Where's that briefcase now, Arnold?"

"To hell with you!" Arnold's voice was shrill, choppy with sudden rage. "Find it, if you're so damned clever!"

"Know where that case went to, Sholtz?" Van demanded.

"I seen him hide it under the instrument cabinet," the con answered, gloatingly. "There's a trick drawer below the bottom shelf."

The Phantom had the briefcase a moment later, was opening it on the operating table, examining its contents, staring keenly at Gimbel's reports on Dr. Hugo Junes' aluminum-calbite fusion experiments.

He studied the reports briefly, then turned to Arnold, and his voice was icy when he spoke. "You intend to talk, Arnold? Or do you think you can hold out?"

"You're not Killer Kline," Arnold snarled abruptly. "You'd be out of here before now, if you were. I got nothing to say, to you or to anybody else. What the hell can you prove, in court?"

"You're in court right now," Van told him tersely, and turned to Sholtz. "Think you can make him talk, if I let you at him?"

"I'll peel him alive if he don't!" the murderer guaranteed, but he eyed Van now with intent sharpness.

Arnold was trying not to show his mounting terror. He glared at Van, stuck to his question: "Sholtz couldn't make me talk. But-who are you?"

For a moment Van hesitated, advancing close to Arnold, And there was something so terrifying in the steely grey eyes boring into the Imperator's that Arnold winced, glanced away, trembling. Van's hand reached down, jerked the ex-Congressman's jaw around so that he couldn't avoid that impelling, piercing stare.

"I'm your judge!" Van said in words that seemed to chill the walls of the concrete room. "I can do with you anything I choose! Arnold, you are facing the Phantom!"

As the dread name filled the strange subterranean room, and the full realization of the power of the man he was up against struck Arnold's consciousness, he slumped back against the wall, seemed suddenly to collapse within himself as a balloon collapses when it is punctured.

Over on the bed, Sholtz began swearing, making low, animal noises, while his eyes, bitter and defeated, stared at the Phantom with a stunned expression of amazed bewilderment.

Harry Arnold's lips moved. His voice came out, dry, grating:

"I've heard-God! I'll talk!"

"I think," Van said flatly, "you're beating Bluebold to the punch. I never met a bull-whip like him yet who wasn't yellow. How'd you happen to pick on him as your right-hand man?"

Arnold's eyes glowered hopelessly. "I had to use him, because of the prison and the men I could take from it. I —"

Arnold, the Imperator, kept on talking, while the Phantom checked his weird, dominion-mad story with Dr. Junes' reports on the operating table, with Sholtz's growled comments, and with his own piecing together of the murderous crime pattern.

The ex-Congressman didn't shut up until, a full hour later, Van unlocked the door and let in Lannigan. With the big Irishman were Bluebold and Dr. Jessup, both handcuffed, Frank Havens, and Colonel Leusik, the tall, sharp-featured National Guard commander.

"Colonel Leusik's men have command of the penitentiary now," Havens said, introducing the colonel and eyeing Van's make-up curiously.

"Lannigan says you have caught the Imperator —" He looked at Arnold and at Sholtz.

The Phantom nodded. "Take the cuffs off Dr. Jessup, if you will, Colonel. I'll try to give you the incriminating facts quickly, since I presume you'll want to turn over the evidence to the governor along with the prisoners. You'll have little difficulty, I'm sure, getting the signatures now of Arnold and Bluebold."

The warden's face whitened and he shot a frantic look toward Arnold. "I'll sign no confession! I'm being railroaded!" He took a menacing step nearer the ex-Congressman. "You-you talked?"

"He beat you there, Bluebold," Van cut in and shoved the big man back against the wall. "You can recriminate after it's over."

Bluebold's jaw dropped as he glared at Van. "Arnold's a liar, whatever he told you! He's behind all this. And you, Killer Kline —"

"The Killer Kline you're looking at," Lannigan said with a growling laugh, "will have to do until the real Kline comes up from Pittsburgh, Bluebold. You signed your death warrant when you signed the commitment papers letting him into your stir!"

The Phantom stepped back to the table, picked up the reports spread there, while the others watched him with mingled emotions.

"As a matter of fact, Bluebold," Van said, "Harry Arnold didn't have to tell me a great deal, although Sholtz and I convinced him it would be a healthy idea. But what he did tell me was startling-the part I couldn't grasp at first:

"Arnold conceived this gigantic idea of the Invisible Empire, gentlemen, not for money. He wanted power. He wanted to be another Hitler, another Mussolini, in America!

"He couldn't do it by votes. He was washed up politically because of a conviction against him in California for an illegal operation on the face of an escaped San Quentin convict. He was known there, he admits, as Dr. Harold Arrnster. His fingerprints and the American Medical Society would have caught up with him if he'd tried to become more than a congressman anywhere in public life.

"But he thought he could get control of the country without votes-by terrorism, by destroying enough well chosen industries and governmental projects, to throw the nation into a helpless, undirected revolt.

"Then he planned to step into control, take over the armed forces with his own trained lieutenants, and set up a new government with himself as dictator."

The Phantom paused, shuffled the reports on the operating table.

"It was the aluminum-calbite fusion experiments of Dr. Hugo Junes at Niagara Falls that first gave me the trail that has ended here in this room, gentlemen! Colonel Leusik, if you'll follow my deductions you'll find the presentation of evidence against Arnold and his assistant, Bluebold, not so complicated.

"I realized, when the Rock Canyon Dam was blown up, that a new explosive had been discovered. For the Arizona dam, and some of the other industrial projects that had been wrecked, had been built to withstand T.N.T. Metallurgical chemistry is a rare enough field, so that any new or outstanding development in it can be traced. Dr. Junes was known to be experimenting with a new metal fusion.

"And then Gimble, carrying a report of Junes' work to Mr. Havens, was shot to death and the reports stolen. I have them here, for they were delivered to Arnold by the killer who escaped.

"Almost immediately, Dr. Junes' experiment blew up in his face. But I'd already realized that, since in all endothermic compounds, terrific heat is necessary to their formation, the sudden releasing of those fused elements, by accident or design, must produce the same amount of heat energy when the elements separate.

"That breakdown makes, rudimentarily, all endothermic explosions, and is the basic rule for the manufacture of trinitrotoluene and the amatol, picric acid and ammoniurn nitrate mixtures we use for blasting and bombs.

"The fusion of aluminum and calbite would be an unstable union, apt to disintegrate in an explosion, without the addition of some stabilizing element. Dr. Junes was using a chip from a meteoric fragment on exhibition at the Smithsonian Institute, so I was sure there'd be an experimental tie-up with that ore.

"There was. The meteorite was a stable fusion of the two metals Junes was trying to unite, But the fusion had happened on another planet. The only way he could find out what the third ingredient was that held them together was by melting them down. And he couldn't do it. The hottest furnaces man had ever made wouldn't do it.

"I had most of this knowledge before meeting Junes. Of course, it was obvious that somebody else was trying to find out what the metallurgist had discovered, how far he'd gone in his fusion, and how close he was to getting sufficient heat to finish his work.

"In fact, the Imperator had his own men working there in Junes' laboratory. And his own metallurgist, the half crazy Vonderkag, was doing things with aluminum and calbite down here underground-things that Junes couldn't do. For Kag had the heat, a natural compressed gas from a subterranean reservoir that would, and did, melt the meteorite and give him the third vital element.

"In the course of Kag's experiments, the metal that Junes was trying to make was perfected. Lannigan found it in discovering the airplane Arnold had got built. But more important, for the Imperator, was Kag's working out of an even higher powered explosive in the disintegration of the new metal.

"It was that latest explosive compound that Arnold relied upon to blast into being his plan for an Invisible Empire that would be no longer invisible but actual and operative. It was the near discovery of that explosive that stopped Junes from continuing his fusion work. He was very close to it then, and saw the danger to the world if such a chemical formula should be perfected."

Van paused again, put down the reports and notes he'd been scanning while he talked.

"I'm telling you this in detail, Colonel," he explained, "because this phase of the investigation won't come out in court. You'll have evidence enough without using it, and it will be better that the public doesn't know of Kag's too dangerous findings. Fortunately, Kag is dead. And the stolen meteorite, along with Dr. Junes' chip from it, have been lost forever in the flooded mine under us.

"And now for the record: It was an accident that Snakey Willow was shot by a New York City detective when Gimble was killed. That was a lead here to this prison —a lead, however, which wouldn't have broken the case. All it would have proved was that one or two convicts had escaped. For Dr. Jessup knew nothing of what was going on, and would have been of no help. Arnold and Bluebold, naturally, would have, and did, cover up nicely any attempt to pry too deeply into their affairs.

"But it wasn't an accident that Arnold and Bluebold were in Frank Havens' office the day Gimble was to have appeared. They were there to see that he didn't get a chance to talk, if Willow and the other gunman missed. And again, Dr. Jessup was brought along as a figure who would help clear them of any suspicion, should there be a slip in their calculations somewhere.

"The chronology of events, Colonel, you can get from Mr. Havens at your leisure. I'm sure he'll help you organize the prosecution against Arnold and Bluebold.

"It was the Imperator's desire to get somebody to replace the erratic and untrustworthy Dr. Vonderkag, that led me here. I submitted to a form of kidnaping, and met Kag. I knew about the stolen meteorite, and was expecting it when it showed up in the underground laboratory under the mines.

"That cinched the location of the Empire and its center as being there. The rest of the job, from my angle, was to force the Imperator into the open. But it wasn't until I tricked him into using me as a murder volunteer that I found this room, and the thermometer with the Alleghany Penitentiary stamp on it. Finding Marks, the Federal agent, a prisoner here, furnished the surgical information needed.

"Thereafter, it was a process of thinning down the suspects up in the prison to a doctor who had the other necessary qualifications to fit the character such a role as the Imperator demanded.

"Death, at the hands of Arnold-although I didn't know who the murderer was at that point-eliminated Vonderkag. It also very nearly eliminated Dr. Jessup, for Jessup would have had to move faster than I'd ever seen him move before, to get in and out of that hospital basement laboratory to kill Kag. Jessup wasn't eliminated then, as a suspect, but my attention turned more suspiciously to the others.

"That brought the choice down to Jessup, Bluebold, Arnold and Rowan, with the emphasis on Bluebold and Arnold. So I cut my thumb with a piece of stiff paper when Jessup and Rowan were occupied phoning. Bluebold was clumsy when he tried to bandage my cut, but Arnold did a very neat spica wrapping—a technique only a doctor or a nurse would be apt to use.

"So I knew that Arnold had once been a medical man. The last move was to force him into the open. I resorted to a bit of ventriloquism, using the radio as a medium and the threat of escaped gas in the mine as a motive for immediate action. The Imperator had to stop that gas-actually, he flooded it out with water, which was the only emergency measure he could take.

"I was ready when he got the lights out, and followed him, with Lannigan. I'd already spotted the water door he'd have to open, down in the mine, so I knew where to catch him. And because of the supposed gas, he'd be wearing a gas mask, which precluded his smelling that there wasn't any leak, and at the same time marked him as the only man in that section of the mine who would not be wearing an Empire face mask.

"There was no difficulty, then, in taking him and bringing him here."

The Phantom smiled thinly, glanced at Bluebold.

The warden was muttering oaths, his eyes glaring at Arnold.

"Bluebold will, I think," Van said drily, "clear up any little details I may have missed."

"By God," the warden exploded. "I heard you! Arnold's talked, you've talked. Damn you, it's my turn now!"

With a slight shrug, Van went to the door, opened it, and stepped out, closing the door upon the violent, cursing recriminations of Black-Jack Bluebold, the Imperator's befuddled lieutenant. Nobody in the room except Lannigan and Havens noticed Van's silent departure.

He used the elevator, got off at the halfway stage, and entered the tunnel, using his deft fingers on his made-up features as he followed the shaft. Killer Kline was disappearing.

When he emerged into the rock quarry, he stood for a moment in the freshness of night, breathing deeply, freeing himself of the atmosphere of the mine.

But it wasn't as Killer Kline that he stared skyward at the silent stars. Nor was it the Phantom who finally lowered his hands from a smudged, rather handsome and weary face. For the Phantom was fading...

Yet a memory that was growing in the strange annals of criminal investigation —a nervous, restless figure in a mask who would, when the vipers of crime bared their poisonous fangs again, stalk once more the dread streets of darkness.

But for the moment, amongst all the teeming millions of the land, there stood alone, here in the quarry, a tall, silent, nondescript figure who was without name, without any tie.

Then that moment was gone. And the lithe form moved swiftly through the shadows of rocks and trees, disappearing toward the road —a road that led back again to the old life and to the Park Avenue penthouse of Richard Curtis Van Loan.

Only a brief sigh that was like a faint, vagrant breeze through the boughs above, signaled the Phantom's transition.

www.ingramcontent.com/pod-product-compliance
Lightning Source LLC
Chambersburg PA
CBHW070807120626
46557CB00002B/745